GOD SEES THE
TRUTH BUT WAITS
and Other Moral Tales

God Sees the Truth but Waits

and Other Moral Tales

DOVER THRIFT EDITIONS

Leo Tolstoy

Edited by

Bob Blaisdell

DOVER PUBLICATIONS
GARDEN CITY, NEW YORK

DOVER THRIFT EDITIONS

GENERAL EDITOR: SUSAN L. RATTINER
EDITOR OF THIS VOLUME: BOB BLAISDELL

This Dover edition, first published in 2024, is a new selection reprinted from
standard texts. A new introduction has been specially prepared for this edition.

Library of Congress Cataloging-in-Publication Data

Names: Tolstoy, Leo, graf, 1828–1910, author. | Blaisdell, Bob, editor.
Title: God sees the truth but waits: and other moral tales / Leo Tolstoy;
   edited by Bob Blaisdell.
Description: Dover edition. | Garden City, New York: Dover Publications,
   2024. | Series: Dover Thrift Editions | Summary: "By the late 1870s, Leo
   Tolstoy had left the Russian Orthodox Church and embarked on a quest for
   spiritual truth, writing profound fable-like short stories. This volume
   features five enlightening tales that exemplify Tolstoy's spiritual
   journey, illuminating the paths to human virtue and salvation"—
   Provided by publisher.
Identifiers: LCCN 2024018056 | ISBN 9780486852430 (trade paperback) | ISBN
   0486852431 (trade paperback)
Subjects: BISAC: FICTION / Religious | FICTION / World Literature / Russia
   / 19th Century | LCGFT: Religious fiction. | Novels.
Classification: LCC PG3366.G64 2024 | DDC 891.73/3—dc23/eng/20240502
LC record available at https://lccn.loc.gov/2024018056

Printed in Canada by Marquis Book
85243101   2024
www.doverpublications.com

Contents

Introduction

LEO TOLSTOY (1828–1910), the most famous Russian author of any century, never stopped searching for the purpose of life and the nature of God.

Tolstoy was born at Yasnaya Polyana, a family estate 120 miles south of Moscow; his mother died before he was two. His father died when he was eight, and he and his siblings were raised by a series of aunts. He started university in Kazan but left before completing a degree. He inherited, as the last son, Yasnaya Polyana, where he started a school for the peasant children and attempted to share the land with his family's serfs. When he was twenty-two, he joined his brother Nikolay, an army officer who was serving in the Caucasus Mountains; while a volunteer in the army, Tolstoy wrote a novella that immediately received acclaim, *Childhood*. He became an army officer in 1852. Though he would become one of the world's most renowned advocates for peace and nonviolent resistance, he was a proud and effective military man. He served until the end of 1856. Before he turned thirty, he was already regarded as a distinctive and important Russian author, but for a few years he threw himself into the study and practice of education; he set up another school for peasant children and opened other free schools in the region. He published a magazine about his school, but when he married in 1862, he gave up teaching and embarked on his historical novel of Russia's resistance to Napoleon's invasion, *War and Peace* (completed in 1869). He and his wife had six children in their first ten years of marriage. Having been long dissatisfied with any of the available materials for teaching reading, Tolstoy decided to create his own series of guides and primers, starting with the alphabet and progressing to two of his most exciting and profound short stories, "A Prisoner in the Caucasus" (1870) and "God Sees the Truth but Waits" (1872).

Though a skeptic of church rituals and a critic of all dogmatism, in the late 1870s, after the exhausting completion of his novel *Anna Karenina*, he attempted to conform himself into a humble adherent of Russian Orthodoxy. He found he could not, however, believe without the use of reason. He left the church and set about studying the Bible on his own. (He had learned Greek and Hebrew.) Though he renounced novel writing (for the time), he set about writing fable-like short stories for the newly literate population. These tales, published in inexpensive booklets, resulted in three of the stories collected here, "What Men Live By" (1881); "Where Love Is, There God Is Also" (1885); and "The Three Hermits" (1886). Each features the miraculous. The final, longest story, "Divine and Human" (1906), is no tale at all but a grim, intense short story based on the lives and activities of two revolutionaries of the late 1870s, in particular the men who were confronting Russia's social injustice with violence and yet, lacking an ultimate truth or God, struggle to find resolution in their own lives.

Tolstoy was excommunicated by the Russian Orthodox Church for his criticisms of their non-Christian applications of power, most importantly support for war and capital punishment. Tolstoy repeatedly declared that he believed in the fundamental truths of Jesus not because Jesus was the son of God, but because the truths that Jesus taught were fundamental to all humankind. It did not matter to Tolstoy, finally, whether any particular divinity existed; he believed that within all people there was a shared recognition of the morality of nonviolence and selflessness.

In the pursuit of truth, in the accomplishment of his worldwide fame as a promoter of nonviolence, he lived in conflict with Russian authorities as well as with his family and wife. When devoted followers of his religious and moral ideas named themselves Tolstoyans, he was for the most part unreceptive to them—for he knew that he himself was *not* a Tolstoyan. He was the long-suffering, long-erring, human Leo Tolstoy. Trying to do good and live by Jesus's principles was his goal, not his unfailing achievement. When Tolstoy died in 1910, he was internationally renowned for his fiction and for his advocacy for peaceful protest.

I have provided short introductory notes to each story as well as the Russian title in Cyrillic if the reader would like to reference the originals in the ninety-volume Soviet edition of Tolstoy's collected works. The translations of the stories based on folk legends, "What Men Live By" and "The Three Hermits," are by Aylmer Maude;

Maude and his wife, the Russian-born Louise Maude, befriended Tolstoy and corresponded with him about some of their translations. Aylmer Maude's excellent biography of Tolstoy was begun before and then revised and completed after Tolstoy's death. "Where Love Is, There God Is Also" has been translated by Leo Wiener, a Russian-born translator of a "Complete" twenty-four-volume translation of Tolstoy's works (1904). Wiener, therefore, did not have access to Tolstoy's not-yet-completed "Divine and Human." There were no translations into English of "Divine and Human" until 2000, when Gordon Spence and Peter Sekirin published their own separate versions. I am grateful to both of those translators for helping popularize this great story in English. Spence's introduction and notes on the historical background of the story are particularly excellent.

I have replaced Maude's British spellings (e.g., "behaviour") with American ones and made occasional adjustments to Maude's and Wiener's paragraph breaks. In translating "God Sees the Truth but Waits," I have benefited from reading and rereading it with my students at Kingsborough Community College (CUNY) in Brooklyn, and then from the most careful and wonderfully patient and astute corrections by the veteran Russian translator Liv Bliss. Bliss also thoroughly corrected my translation of "Divine and Human," helping make the long story scrupulously faithful to the Russian and more natural to the English. I also thank Anna Schott, Kia Penso, Max Blaisdell, and Suzanne Carbotte for reading and commenting on earlier drafts of "Divine and Human." Professor Michael Denner, editor of *Tolstoy Studies Journal*, suggested background readings about that story. The most informative and compelling commentaries on "God Sees the Truth but Waits," by Hugh McLean and Gary Jahn, can be found in Professor McLean's *In Quest of Tolstoy* (2008). I learned details of the other stories' histories from the editors of Tolstoy's complete works, that is, *Polnoe Sobranie Sochinenii* (Moscow and Leningrad, 1928–64), and the *L. N. Tolstoy Entsyklopediya,* edited by Nina Il'darovna Burnasheva (Moscow, 2009). Finally, I thank Fiona Hallowell at Dover Publications for her kind support and encouragement of this project.

—*Bob Blaisdell*

GOD SEES THE TRUTH BUT WAITS

and Other Moral Tales

Tolstoy believed this tale ("Бог Правду Видитъ, Да Не Скоро Скажетъ"[1]) was his only work that achieved the supreme level of art.[2] This translation uses his original, painstakingly revised version, the crowning story in his children's primer, Azbuka (1872). It did make its first appearance in the magazine Conversation earlier that year, and a shorter version of the tale is told by the character Platon Karataev in 1869's War and Peace.[3]

The title comes from a Russian proverb, a form of folk wisdom Tolstoy loved. The humbled, wrongfully accused hero Ivan Dmitrievich Aksenov realizes that "other than God, no one can know the truth, and He alone must be entreated and from Him alone can mercy be expected."

1

God Sees the Truth but Waits

IN THE TOWN of Vladimir there lived a young merchant, Aksenov. He owned two shops and a house. In looks, Aksenov was handsome,

---

[1] The title is more literally but less well known as "God Sees the Right, Though He Be Slow to Declare It," as Nathan Haskell Dole rendered it in 1910.

[2] In 1898's *What Is Art?* (translated by Aylmer Maude), Tolstoy writes: "I consign my own artistic productions to the category of bad art, excepting 'God Sees the Truth.'"

[3] Tolstoy almost always defied editorial suggestions of changes while he was still actively engaged with the writing, but he was relatively indifferent to modifications or adaptations afterward. In 1885, Tolstoy allowed his friend Vladimir Chertkov to revise one moment of the story wherein the story's hero, Aksenov, tells a deliberate lie; later, Aylmer Maude made, with Tolstoy's acceptance, another small alteration in a detail. Those changes have been ignored in this translation.

with light-brown, curly hair, and he made merry and sang like no other. When younger, Aksenov had done a lot of drinking, and when he got drunk, he got rowdy, but ever since he married he had given up drinking, except on rare occasions.

Once, in summer time, Aksenov was going to Nizhny, to the fair. As he began to say goodbye to his family, his wife said to him, "Ivan Dmitrievich, don't go today. I've had a bad dream about you."

Aksenov laughed and said, "Are you still afraid that I'll go on a bender at the fair?"

His wife said, "I don't know myself what I'm afraid of, but what I dreamt was so bad. I dreamt that you came back from the city and took off your cap, and what do I see? Your head's all gray."

Aksenov burst out laughing. "Well, that means profit. Just see, I'll sell all my goods and bring back some expensive presents."

And he bade his family goodbye and left.

Halfway there, he came upon a merchant he knew, and they stopped together for the night. They drank tea together and lay down to sleep in two adjoining rooms. Aksenov didn't like sleeping long; he woke up in the middle of the night, and, because it was easier to travel in the cool, he roused the driver and told him to harness the horses. Then he went to the landlord's quarters, settled the bill with him and left.

Having gone about twenty-five miles, he again stopped to feed the horses and to rest in the post-yard hallway; at lunch time, he went onto the porch and ordered the samovar to be set up; he took a guitar and began playing. Suddenly, a troika with bells pulled into the yard, and an official got out of the cart with two soldiers, came up to Aksenov and asked, "Who are you? Where are you from?" Aksenov told all as it was and asked, "Would you care to take tea with me?"

But the official still beset him with questions: "Where did you spend last night? Alone or with a merchant? Did you see the merchant this morning? Why did you leave the post-yard so early?"

Aksenov wondered why he was being asked all this; he had told everything as it was, and so he said, "Why do you question me this way? I'm neither a thief nor some kind of outlaw. I'm traveling on my own business, and there's nothing to ask me about."

That was when the official called over the soldiers and said, "I'm the police superintendent, and I'm questioning you because the merchant with whom you spent last night has had his throat cut. Show me your things—and you men, search him."

They went into the hut, took his case and bag and began undoing them and searching. Suddenly the superintendent pulled a knife out of the bag and shouted, "Whose knife is this?"

Aksenov looked and saw that a bloody knife had been taken out of his bag and was afraid.

"And why is there blood on the knife?"

Aksenov wanted to answer, but he couldn't get the words out. "I … I don't know … I … knife … I … not mine …"

Then the superintendent said, "Come morning, the merchant was found in bed with his throat cut. Other than you, no one could have done it. The hut was locked from the inside, and there was no one other than you in the hut. Here's a bloody knife in your bag, and by your face it's clear to see. Say how you killed him and how much money you stole."

Aksenov swore to God that it wasn't he who had done it, that he hadn't seen the merchant after drinking tea with him, that the money was only his own eight thousand, that the knife wasn't his. But his voice faltered, his face was pale, and he was shaking all over from fear, like a guilty man.

The superintendent called the soldiers and ordered them to tie him up and take him to the cart. When they were hoisting him into the cart with his legs bound, Aksenov crossed himself and began to weep. They took Aksenov's things and his money, and dispatched him to a stockade in a nearby town. They sent off to Vladimir to find out what kind of person Aksenov was, and all the merchants and the people of Vladimir testified that when younger, Aksenov drank and caroused but was a good person. Then they began to pass judgment on him. They passed judgment on him for killing the merchant from Ryazan and stealing 20,000 rubles.

His wife was grieving over her husband and didn't know what to think. Her children were all still little, and one was at the breast. She gathered them all up with her and traveled to the town where her husband was being held in the stockade. At first they wouldn't admit her, but then she implored the authorities, and she was brought to her husband. When she saw him in prison garb, in chains, in the company of outlaws—she collapsed to the ground and for a long time couldn't come to herself. Then she arranged her children around her, sat alongside him, and began telling him about things at home and asking him about all that had happened to him. He told her everything. She said, "And what now?"

He said, "We must petition the tsar. An innocent man cannot perish!"

His wife said that she had already sent a petition to the tsar, but that the petition had not reached him. Aksenov said nothing and only lowered his eyes. Then his wife said, "It wasn't for nothing then, you remember, that I dreamt you'd gone gray. Here you really have gone gray from sorrow. If only you hadn't set out back then."

And she began running her fingers through his hair and said, "Vanya, my beloved, tell your wife the truth: You didn't do it, did you?"

Aksenov said, "And you think that of me?" He covered his face with his hands and began to weep. Then a soldier came and said that his wife and children had to leave. And for the last time, Aksenov said goodbye to his family.

When his wife had left, Aksenov began recalling what had been said. When he remembered that his wife also thought that of him and was asking if he had killed the merchant, he said to himself, "It's clear to see that, other than God, no one can know the truth, and He alone must be entreated and from Him alone can mercy be expected." From then on, Aksenov stopped sending petitions, stopped hoping and only prayed to God.

Aksenov was sentenced to be punished with the knout, and then exiled to hard labor. So it was done. They whipped him with the knout, and then, when the wounds from the knout healed, he was herded off with other convicts to Siberia.

In Siberia, at hard labor, Aksenov lived for twenty-six years. The hair on his head turned white as snow, and his beard grew out long, narrow and gray. All of his cheerfulness disappeared. He stooped, began to walk slowly, spoke little, never laughed and often prayed to God.

In the stockade, Aksenov learned to make boots, and with his earnings he bought *Lives of the Saints* and read it when there was light in the prison; on feast days, he went to the prison church, read the Epistles and sang in the choir—his voice was still good. The authorities loved Aksenov for his humility, and his prison-mates respected him and called him "gramps" and "man of God." When there were favors to ask in the prison, his comrades always sent Aksenov to petition the authorities, and when there were quarrels among the convicts, they always came to Aksenov to settle them.

No one wrote letters to Aksenov from home, and he didn't know if his wife and children were alive.

One day new prisoners were brought to serve at hard labor. In the evening all the old prisoners gathered around the newcomers and started questioning them on which town or village they were from and what charges had been brought against them. Aksenov also sat on the cot near the newcomers and, eyes cast down, listened to their stories. One of the new prisoners was a tall, hardy old fellow of about sixty with a gray, clipped beard. He was telling what they had caught him for.

He said, "So, brothers, it was for nothing that I landed here. I untied a driver's horse from its sleigh. They arrested me, saying I stole it. And I say, 'I only wanted to get there faster—I let the horse go. And the driver's a pal of mine. So everything's in order?' I say. 'No,' they say. 'You stole it.' But they didn't know what I'd really stolen or where. There were things that should have landed me here long ago, but they couldn't catch me out, and now, contrary to the law, they've driven me here. And I'm lying: I've been in Siberia before, but didn't stay long …"

"And where would you be from?" asked one of the prisoners.

"From the town of Vladimir I am—a registered townsman. I'm Makar by name but am styled Semenovich."

Aksenov raised his head and asked, "But might you have heard, Semenich, of the Aksenov merchants in Vladimir? Are they alive?"

"How would I not hear? Rich merchants they are, for all that the father's in Siberia. It's clear to see that he's a sinner such as we. And you, gramps, on what charge are you here?"

Aksenov didn't like talking about his misfortune; he sighed and said, "For my sins I have found myself here at hard labor for twenty-six years."

Makar Semenov said, "For what sins?"

Aksenov said, "I must have deserved it," and he didn't want to tell any more, but the other prison comrades told the newcomer how Aksenov had landed in Siberia. They told how someone killed a merchant on the road and planted a knife on Aksenov, and how for this he was wrongly sentenced.

When Makar Semenov heard this, he glanced at Aksenov, clapped his hands on his knees, and said, "What a miracle! Here's a miracle! But how you've aged, gramps!"

They began asking him why he was surprised and where he had seen Aksenov; but Makar Semenov didn't answer and only said, "It's miraculous, lads, for us to meet here!"

And from these words the thought came to Aksenov that this fellow might know who killed the merchant. He said, "Either you've heard, Semenich, about this matter before, or you've seen me before."

"How could I not hear! The world's full of rumors. But that's already long ago. What I heard I've forgotten," said Makar Semenov.

"Maybe you heard who killed the merchant?" asked Aksenov.

Makar Semenov laughed and said, "But it's clear to see that the one who killed him was the one in whose bag the knife was found. If somebody planted a knife on you and wasn't caught, then he's no thief. And anyway how'd he put the knife into your bag? Wasn't it under your head? You'd have heard something."

As soon as Aksenov heard these words, he thought that this was the very man who had killed the merchant. He stood up and stepped away. Aksenov couldn't fall asleep all night. Longing overwhelmed him, and images came to his mind: first he imagined his wife as she was when she bade him farewell for the last time, on his way to the fair. Then he saw her as if she were there in life, and he could see her face and eyes, and could hear her talk and laugh. Then he imagined his children as they were then—small, one in a little coat, one at the breast. And he remembered himself as he was then—joyful, young. He remembered sitting on the porch at the post-yard where they arrested him, and playing a guitar, and how joyful his soul was back then. And he remembered the pillory where they flogged him and the executioner, and the people around, and the chains, and the prisoners, and all the twenty-six years of prison life, and he remembered his old age. And such longing overwhelmed Aksenov that he would gladly have laid hands on himself.

"And all because of this villain!" thought Aksenov.

Such rage at Makar Semenov overwhelmed him that, even if it would be the death of him, he wanted to take revenge. He prayed all night, but he couldn't calm down. During the day he didn't approach Makar Semenov and didn't look at him.

So passed two weeks. Aksenov couldn't sleep at night, and such longing overwhelmed him that he didn't know what to do with himself.

One night he went walking through the prison and saw that earth was being dug up under one of the cots. He stopped to watch. Suddenly Makar Semenov jumped up from under the cot and with a frightened face glanced at Aksenov. Aksenov wanted to pass by so as not to see him, but Makar grabbed him by the arm and told him that he was digging a passage under the walls and that he was carrying the dirt out every day in his boots and scattering it along the street when they were being sent out to work.

He said, "Just keep quiet, old man, and I'll bring you out too. But if you say anything, they'll flog me, and I won't let you off either—I'll kill you."

When Aksenov saw this one who had done him wrong, he began to shake all over with fury, pulled his arm away and said, "I have no cause to get out, and there is no reason to kill me—you killed me long ago. Whether I tell them about you or not, that will be as God lays on my soul."

The next day, when the convicts were being led out to work, the soldiers noticed the dirt that Makar Semenov had scattered,[4] and they began searching the prison and found the hole. The commandant arrived at the prison and began asking everyone, "Who dug the hole?"

Everybody denied any knowledge. Those who knew didn't give Makar Semenov away, because they knew that he would be flogged almost to death for it. Then the commandant turned to Aksenov. He knew that Aksenov was a fair-minded man, and said, "Old man, you're truthful; tell me, before God, who did this?"

Makar Semenov was standing there as if nothing was wrong and looking at the commandant, and didn't glance over at Aksenov. Aksenov's hands and lips trembled, and for a long while he couldn't utter a word. He was thinking, "If I give him cover, why am I forgiving him, when he has ruined me? Let him pay for my torment. But if I tell them it was he, that's it—they'll flog him. And suppose what I think of him is mistaken? And what then—how would that be easier on me?"

The commandant asked once more, "Well, what then will it be, old man? Speak the truth: who was digging?"

Aksenov gave Makar Semenov a glance and said, "I didn't see, and I don't know."

So they didn't find out who had done the digging.

The next night, when Aksenov had lain down on his cot and was dozing off, he heard that someone had come up and had sat at his feet. He looked into the darkness and recognized Makar.

---

[4] "[…] солдаты примѣтили, что Макаръ Семёновъ высыпалъ землю […]"
Literally: "the soldiers noticed that Makar Semenov had scattered the dirt." In English, that sounds as if the soldiers noticed Makar doing it, and if so, they would have nabbed him right then. I have clarified (or corrected) the phrasing. [Translator.]

Aksenov said, "What more do you want from me? What are you doing here?"

Makar Semenov was silent. Aksenov sat up and said, "What do you want? Go away or I'll call for a soldier."

Makar Semenov leaned in close to Aksenov and in a whisper said, "Ivan Dmitrievich, forgive me!"

Aksenov said, "Forgive you for what?"

"I killed the merchant, and I planted the knife on you. I wanted to kill you too, but there were sounds in the yard. I put the knife in your bag and climbed out the window."

Aksenov was silent and didn't know what to say. Makar Semenov got off the cot, bowed to the ground, and said, "Ivan Dmitrievich, forgive me, forgive, for God's sake. I'll confess that I killed the merchant—they'll pardon you. You'll return home."

Aksenov said, "That's easy for you to say, but however will I bear it? Where will I go now? … My wife has died; my children have forgotten me; I have nowhere to go …"

Makar Semenov did not get up from the floor; he beat his head on the ground and said, "Ivan Dmitrich, forgive me! When they flogged me with the knout, it was easier for me than it is to look at you now … And still you took pity on me—you didn't tell. Forgive me, for Christ's sake. Forgive me, damned villain that I am!" And he began to sob.

When Aksenov heard that Makar Semenov was weeping, he himself began to weep and said, "God will forgive you; maybe I'm a hundred times worse than you!"[5]

And suddenly, his soul became easy. He stopped longing for home, and he didn't want to leave the prison, but only thought about his last hour.

Makar Semenov didn't heed Aksenov and confessed his guilt. When the decision was issued to let Aksenov return, Aksenov had already died.

(1872)
Translated by Bob Blaisdell

---

[5] Aylmer Maude notes that in Tolstoy's play *The Power of Darkness*: "A formal request for forgiveness is customary among Russians, but it is often no mere formality. … his second reply, 'God will forgive you,' is the correct one sanctioned by custom."

Tolstoy learned this story ("Чем Люди Живы") from the wandering peasant storyteller Vasily Petrovich Shchegolenok, and adapted it, in thirty-three drafts, in his own dynamic and thorough way. He initially titled it "The Angel on Earth." The first publication of the story was in 1881 in a children's magazine.

The angel Michael, punished by God for disobedience, must suffer in human form until he learns the three truths of "What Men Live By": "I have now understood that though it seems to men that they live by care for themselves, in truth it is love alone by which they live. He who has love, is in God, and God is in him, for God is love." Note that the "men" should be taken to mean "people." Finally, the editor of this volume recommends, for the sake of comparison and contrast, an adaptation of the story by Alexander Kushnir in his 2008 short film, "What Men Live By. With English subtitles. Chem ludi zhivy," on YouTube.

2

What Men Live By

"We know that we have passed out of death into life, because we love the brethren. He that loveth not abideth in death."
—1 *Epistle St. John* iii. 14.

"Whoso hath the world's goods, and beholdeth his brother in need, and shutteth up his compassion from him, how doth the love of God abide in him? My little children, let us not love in word, neither with the tongue; but in deed and truth."
—iii. 17–18.

"Love is of God; and every one that loveth is begotten of God, and knoweth God. He that loveth not knoweth not God; for God is love."—iv. 7–8.

"No man hath beheld God at any time; if we love one another, God abideth in us."—iv. 12.

"God is love; and he that abideth in love abideth in God, and God abideth in him."—iv. 16.

"If a man say, I love God, and hateth his brother, he is a liar; for he that loveth not his brother whom he hath seen, how can he love God whom he hath not seen?"—iv. 20.[6]

I.

A SHOEMAKER NAMED Simon, who had neither house nor land of his own, lived with his wife and children in a peasant's hut, and earned his living by his work. Work was cheap, but bread was dear, and what he earned he spent for food. The man and his wife had but one sheepskin coat between them for winter wear, and even that was torn to tatters, and this was the second year he had been wanting to buy sheep-skins for a new coat. Before winter Simon saved up a little money: a three-ruble note lay hidden in his wife's box, and five rubles and twenty kopeks were owed him by customers in the village.

So one morning he prepared to go to the village to buy the sheep-skins. He put on over his shirt his wife's wadded nankeen jacket, and over that he put his own cloth coat. He took the three-ruble note in his pocket, cut himself a stick to serve as a staff, and started off after breakfast. "I'll collect the five rubles that are due to me," thought he, "add the three I have got, and that will be enough to buy sheep-skins for the winter coat."

He came to the village and called at a peasant's hut, but the man was not at home. The peasant's wife promised that the money should be paid next week, but she would not pay it herself. Then Simon called on another peasant, but this one swore he had no money, and would only pay twenty kopeks which he owed for a pair of boots Simon had mended. Simon then tried to buy the sheep-skins on credit, but the dealer would not trust him.

"Bring your money," said he, "then you may have your pick of the skins. We know what debt-collecting is like." So all the business the shoemaker did was to get the twenty kopeks for boots he had mended, and to take a pair of felt boots a peasant gave him to sole with leather.

---

[6] Aylmer Maude lightly adapts the King James Version of the Bible.

Simon felt downhearted. He spent the twenty kopeks on vodka, and started homewards without having bought any skins. In the morning he had felt the frost; but now, after drinking the vodka, he felt warm, even without a sheep-skin coat. He trudged along, striking his stick on the frozen earth with one hand, swinging the felt boots with the other, and talking to himself.

"I'm quite warm," said he, "though I have no sheep-skin coat. I've had a drop, and it runs through all my veins. I need no sheep-skins. I go along and don't worry about anything. That's the sort of man I am! What do I care? I can live without sheep-skins. I don't need them. My wife will fret, to be sure. And, true enough, it is a shame; one works all day long, and then does not get paid. Stop a bit! If you don't bring that money along, sure enough I'll skin you, blessed if I don't. How's that? He pays twenty kopeks at a time! What can I do with twenty kopeks? Drink it—that's all one can do! Hard up, he says he is! So he may be—but what about me? You have a house, and cattle, and everything; I've only what I stand up in! You have corn of your own growing; I have to buy every grain. Do what I will, I must spend three rubles every week for bread alone. I come home and find the bread all used up, and I have to fork out another ruble and a half. So just pay up what you owe, and no nonsense about it!"

By this time he had nearly reached the shrine at the bend of the road. Looking up, he saw something whitish behind the shrine. The daylight was fading, and the shoemaker peered at the thing without being able to make out what it was. "There was no white stone here before. Can it be an ox? It's not like an ox. It has a head like a man, but it's too white; and what could a man be doing there?"

He came closer, so that it was clearly visible. To his surprise it really was a man, alive or dead, sitting naked, leaning motionless against the shrine. Terror seized the shoemaker, and he thought, "Someone has killed him, stripped him, and left him there. If I meddle I shall surely get into trouble."

So the shoemaker went on. He passed in front of the shrine so that he could not see the man. When he had gone some way, he looked back, and saw that the man was no longer leaning against the shrine, but was moving as if looking towards him. The shoemaker felt more frightened than before, and thought, "Shall I go back to him, or shall I go on? If I go near him something dreadful may happen. Who knows who the fellow is? He has not come here for any good. If I go near him he may jump up and throttle me, and there will be no getting away. Or if not, he'd still be a burden on one's hands. What could I do with a naked man? I couldn't give him my last clothes. Heaven only help me to get away!"

So the shoemaker hurried on, leaving the shrine behind him—when suddenly his conscience smote him, and he stopped in the road.

"What are you doing, Simon?" said he to himself. "The man may be dying of want, and you slip past afraid. Have you grown so rich as to be afraid of robbers? Ah, Simon, shame on you!"

So he turned back and went up to the man.

II.

SIMON APPROACHED THE stranger, looked at him, and saw that he was a young man, fit, with no bruises on his body, only evidently freezing and frightened, and he sat there leaning back without looking up at Simon, as if too faint to lift his eyes. Simon went close to him, and then the man seemed to wake up. Turning his head, he opened his eyes and looked into Simon's face. That one look was enough to make Simon fond of the man. He threw the felt boots on the ground, undid his sash, laid it on the boots, and took off his cloth coat.

"It's not a time for talking," said he. "Come, put this coat on at once!" And Simon took the man by the elbows and helped him to rise. As he stood there, Simon saw that his body was clean and in good condition, his hands and feet shapely, and his face good and kind. He threw his coat over the man's shoulders, but the latter could not find the sleeves. Simon guided his arms into them, and drawing the coat well on, wrapped it closely about him, tying the sash round the man's waist.

Simon even took off his torn cap to put it on the man's head, but then his own head felt cold, and he thought: "I'm quite bald, while he has long curly hair." So he put his cap on his own head again. "It will be better to give him something for his feet," thought he; and he made the man sit down, and helped him to put on the felt boots, saying, "There, friend, now move about and warm yourself. Other matters can be settled later on. Can you walk?"

The man stood up and looked kindly at Simon, but could not say a word.

"Why don't you speak?" said Simon. "It's too cold to stay here, we must be getting home. There now, take my stick, and if you're feeling weak, lean on that. Now step out!"

The man started walking, and moved easily, not lagging behind.

As they went along, Simon asked him, "And where do you belong to?"

"I'm not from these parts."

"I thought as much. I know the folks hereabouts. But, how did you come to be there by the shrine?"

"I cannot tell."

"Has someone been ill-treating you?"

"No one has ill-treated me. God has punished me."

"Of course God rules all. Still, you'll have to find food and shelter somewhere. Where do you want to go to?"

"It is all the same to me."

Simon was amazed. The man did not look like a rogue, and he spoke gently, but yet he gave no account of himself. Still Simon thought, "Who knows what may have happened?" And he said to the stranger: "Well then, come home with me, and at least warm yourself awhile."

So Simon walked towards his home, and the stranger kept up with him, walking at his side. The wind had risen and Simon felt it cold under his shirt. He was getting over his tipsiness by now, and began to feel the frost. He went along sniffling and wrapping his wife's coat round him, and he thought to himself: "There now—talk about sheep-skins! I went out for sheep-skins and come home without even a coat to my back, and what is more, I'm bringing a naked man along with me. Matryona won't be pleased!" And when he thought of his wife he felt sad; but when he looked at the stranger and remembered how he had looked up at him at the shrine, his heart was glad.

III.

Simon's wife had everything ready early that day. She had cut wood, brought water, fed the children, eaten her own meal, and now she sat thinking. She wondered when she ought to make bread: now or tomorrow? There was still a large piece left.

"If Simon has had some dinner in town," thought she, "and does not eat much for supper, the bread will last out another day."

She weighed the piece of bread in her hand again and again, and thought: "I won't make any more today. We have only enough flour left to bake one batch; We can manage to make this last out till Friday."

So Matryona put away the bread, and sat down at the table to patch her husband's shirt. While she worked she thought how her husband was buying skins for a winter coat.

"If only the dealer does not cheat him. My good man is much too simple; he cheats nobody, but any child can take him in. Eight rubles is a lot of money—he should get a good coat at that price. Not tanned skins, but still a proper winter coat. How difficult it was last winter to get on without a warm coat. I could neither get down to the river, nor go out anywhere. When he went out he put on all we had, and there was nothing left for me. He did not start very early today, but still it's time he was back. I only hope he has not gone on a bender!"

Hardly had Matryona thought this, when steps were heard on the threshold, and someone entered. Matryona stuck her needle into her work and went out into the passage. There she saw two men: Simon, and with him a man without a hat, and wearing felt boots.

Matryona noticed at once that her husband smelt of spirits. "There now, he has been drinking," thought she. And when she saw that he was coatless, had only her jacket on, brought no parcel, stood there silent, and seemed ashamed, her heart was ready to break with disappointment. "He has drunk the money," thought she, "and has been on a bender with some good-for-nothing fellow whom he has brought home with him."

Matryona let them pass into the hut, followed them in, and saw that the stranger was a young, slight man, wearing her husband's coat. There was no shirt to be seen under it, and he had no hat. Having entered, he stood, neither moving, nor raising his eyes, and Matryona thought: "He must be a bad man—he's afraid."

Matryona frowned, and stood beside the oven looking to see what they would do.

Simon took off his cap and sat down on the bench as if things were all right.

"Come, Matryona; if supper is ready, let us have some."

Matryona muttered something to herself and did not move, but stayed where she was, by the oven. She looked first at the one and then at the other of them, and only shook her head. Simon saw that his wife was annoyed, but tried to pass it off. Pretending not to notice anything, he took the stranger by the arm.

"Sit down, friend," said he, "and let us have some supper."

The stranger sat down on the bench.

"Haven't you cooked anything for us?" said Simon.

Matryona's anger boiled over. "I've cooked, but not for you. It seems to me you have drunk your wits away. You went to buy a sheep-skin coat, but come home without so much as the coat you had on, and bring a naked vagabond home with you. I have no supper for drunkards like you."

"That's enough, Matryona. Don't wag your tongue without reason. You had better ask what sort of man—"

"And you tell me what you've done with the money?"

Simon found the pocket of the jacket, drew out the three-ruble note, and unfolded it.

"Here is the money. Trifonof did not pay, but promises to pay soon."

Matryona got still more angry; he had bought no sheep-skins, but had put his only coat on some naked fellow and had even brought him to their house.

She snatched up the note from the table, took it to put away in safety, and said: "I have no supper for you. We can't feed all the naked drunkards in the world."

"There now, Matryona, hold your tongue a bit. First hear what a man has to say—"

"Much wisdom I shall hear from a drunken fool. I was right in not wanting to marry you—a drunkard. The linen my mother gave me you drank; and now you've been to buy a coat—and have drunk it, too!"

Simon tried to explain to his wife that he had only spent twenty kopeks; tried to tell how he had found the man—but Matryona would not let him get a word in. She talked nineteen to the dozen, and dragged in things that had happened ten years before.

Matryona talked and talked, and at last she flew at Simon and seized him by the sleeve.

"Give me my jacket. It is the only one I have, and you must needs take it from me and wear it yourself. Give it here, you mangy dog, and may the devil take you."

Simon began to pull off the jacket, and turned a sleeve of it inside out; Matryona seized the jacket and it burst its seams, She snatched it up, threw it over her head and went to the door. She meant to go out, but stopped undecided—she wanted to work off her anger, but she also wanted to learn what sort of a man the stranger was.

IV.

Matryona stopped and said: "If he were a good man he would not be naked. Why, he hasn't even a shirt on him. If he were all right, you would say where you came across the fellow."

"That's just what I am trying to tell you," said Simon. "As I came to the shrine I saw him sitting all naked and frozen. It isn't quite the weather to sit about naked! God sent me to him, or he would have perished. What was I to do? How do we know what may have happened to him? So I took him, clothed him, and brought him along. Don't be so angry, Matryona. It is a sin. Remember, we all must die one day."

Angry words rose to Matryona's lips, but she looked at the stranger and was silent. He sat on the edge of the bench, motionless, his hands folded on his knees, his head drooping on his breast, his eyes closed, and his brows knit as if in pain. Matryona was silent: and Simon said: "Matryona, have you no love of God?"

Matryona heard these words, and as she looked at the stranger, suddenly her heart softened towards him. She came back from the door, and going to the oven she got out the supper. Setting a cup on the table, she poured out some kvas. Then she brought out the last piece of bread, and set out a knife and spoons.

"Eat, if you want to," said she.

Simon drew the stranger to the table.

"Take your place, young man," said he.

Simon cut the bread, crumbled it into the broth, and they began to eat. Matryona sat at the corner of the table resting her head on her hand and looking at the stranger.

And Matryona was touched with pity for the stranger, and began to feel fond of him. And at once the stranger's face lit up; his brows were no longer bent, he raised his eyes and smiled at Matryona.

When they had finished supper, the woman cleared away the things and began questioning the stranger. "Where are you from?" said she.

"I am not from these parts."

"But how did you come to be on the road?"

"I may not tell."

"Did someone rob you?"

"God punished me."

"And you were lying there naked?"

"Yes, naked and freezing. Simon saw me and had pity on me. He took off his coat, put it on me and brought me here. And you have fed me, given me drink, and shown pity on me. God will reward you!"

Matryona rose, took from the window Simon's old shirt she had been patching, and gave it to the stranger. She also brought out a pair of trousers for him.

"There," said she, "I see you have no shirt. Put this on, and lie down where you please, in the loft or on the oven."[7]

The stranger took off the coat, put on the shirt, and lay down in the loft. Matryona put out the candle, took the coat, and climbed to where her husband lay.

Matryona drew the skirts of the coat over her and lay down, but could not sleep; she could not get the stranger out of her mind.

When she remembered that he had eaten their last piece of bread and that there was none for tomorrow, and thought of the shirt and trousers she had given away, she felt grieved; but when she remembered how he had smiled, her heart was glad.

Long did Matryona lie awake, and she noticed that Simon also was awake—he drew the coat towards him.

"Simon!"

"Well?"

"You have had the last of the bread, and I have not put any to rise. I don't know what we shall do tomorrow. Perhaps I can borrow some of neighbor Martha."

"If we're alive we shall find something to eat."

The woman lay still awhile, and then said, "He seems a good man, but why does he not tell us who he is?"

"I suppose he has his reasons."

"Simon!"

"Well?"

"We give; but why does nobody give us anything?"

Simon did not know what to say; so he only said, "Let us stop talking," and turned over and went to sleep.

---

[7] In a Russian peasant hut, there was usually a sleeping shelf built atop the wide, hearth-like oven.

V.

IN THE MORNING Simon awoke. The children were still asleep; his wife had gone to the neighbor's to borrow some bread. The stranger alone was sitting on the bench, dressed in the old shirt and trousers, and looking upwards. His face was brighter than it had been the day before.

Simon said to him, "Well, friend; the belly wants bread, and the naked body clothes. One has to work for a living What work do you know?"

"I do not know any."

This surprised Simon, but he said, "Men who want to learn can learn anything."

"Men work, and I will work also."

"What is your name?"

"Michael."

"Well, Michael, if you don't wish to talk about yourself, that is your own affair; but you'll have to earn a living for yourself. If you will work as I tell you, I will give you food and shelter."

"May God reward you! I will learn. Show me what to do."

Simon took yarn, put it round his thumb and began to twist it.

"It is easy enough—see!"

Michael watched him, put some yarn round his own thumb in the same way, caught the knack, and twisted the yarn also.

Then Simon showed him how to wax the thread. This also Michael mastered. Next Simon showed him how to twist the bristle in, and how to sew, and this, too, Michael learned at once.

Whatever Simon showed him he understood at once, and after three days he worked as if he had sewn boots all his life. He worked without stopping, and ate little. When work was over he sat silently, looking upwards. He hardly went into the street, spoke only when necessary, and neither joked nor laughed. They never saw him smile, except that first evening when Matryona gave them supper.

VI.

DAY BY DAY and week by week the year went round. Michael lived and worked with Simon. His fame spread till people said that no one sewed boots so neatly and strongly as Simon's workman, Michael; and from all the district round people came to Simon for their boots, and he began to be well off.

One winter day, as Simon and Michael sat working, a carriage on sledge-runners, with three horses and with bells, drove up to the hut. They looked out of the window; the carriage stopped at their door, a fine servant jumped down from the box and opened the door. A gentleman in a fur coat got out and walked up to Simon's hut. Up jumped Matryona and opened the door wide. The gentleman stooped to enter the hut, and when he drew himself up again his head nearly reached the ceiling, and he seemed quite to fill his end of the room.

Simon rose, bowed, and looked at the gentleman with astonishment. He had never seen anyone like him. Simon himself was lean, Michael was thin, and Matryona was dry as a bone, but this man was like someone from another world: red-faced, burly, with a neck like a bull's, and looking altogether as if he were cast in iron.

The gentleman puffed, threw off his fur coat, sat down on the bench, and said, "Which of you is the master bootmaker?"

"I am, your Excellency," said Simon, coming forward.

Then the gentleman shouted to his lad, "Hey, Fedka, bring the leather!"

The servant ran in, bringing a parcel. The gentleman took the parcel and put it on the table.

"Untie it," said he. The lad untied it.

The gentleman pointed to the leather.

"Look here, shoemaker," said he, "do you see this leather?"

"Yes, your honor."

"But do you know what sort of leather it is?"

Simon felt the leather and said, "It is good leather."

"Good, indeed! Why, you fool, you never saw such leather before in your life. It's German, and cost twenty rubles."

Simon was frightened, and said, "Where should I ever see leather like that?"

"Just so! Now, can you make it into boots for me?"

"Yes, your Excellency, I can."

Then the gentleman shouted at him: "You can, can you? Well, remember whom you are to make them for, and what the leather is. You must make me boots that will wear for a year, neither losing shape nor coming unsown. If you can do it, take the leather and cut it up; but if you can't, say so. I warn you now if your boots become unsewn or lose shape within a year, I will have you put in prison. If they don't burst or lose shape for a year I will pay you ten rubles for your work."

Simon was frightened, and did not know what to say. He glanced at Michael and nudging him with his elbow, whispered: "Shall I take the work?"

Michael nodded his head as if to say, "Yes, take it."

Simon did as Michael advised, and undertook to make boots that would not lose shape or split for a whole year.

Calling his servant, the gentleman told him to pull the boot off his left leg, which he stretched out.

"Take my measure!" said he.

Simon stitched a paper measure seventeen inches long, smoothed it out, knelt down, wiped his hand well on his apron so as not to soil the gentleman's sock, and began to measure. He measured the sole, and round the instep, and began to measure the calf of the leg, but the paper was too short. The calf of the leg was as thick as a beam.

"Mind you don't make it too tight in the leg."

Simon stitched on another strip of paper. The gentleman twitched his toes about in his sock, looking round at those in the hut, and as he did so he noticed Michael.

"Whom have you there?" asked he.

"That is my workman. He will sew the boots."

"Mind," said the gentleman to Michael, "remember to make them so that they will last me a year."

Simon also looked at Michael, and saw that Michael was not looking at the gentleman, but was gazing into the corner behind the gentleman, as if he saw someone there. Michael looked and looked, and suddenly he smiled, and his face became brighter.

"What are you grinning at, you fool?" thundered the gentleman. "You had better look to it that the boots are ready in time."

"They shall be ready in good time," said Michael.

"Mind it is so," said the gentleman, and he put on his boots and his fur coat, wrapped the latter round him, and went to the door. But he forgot to stoop, and struck his head against the lintel.

He swore and rubbed his head. Then he took his seat in the carriage and drove away.

When he had gone, Simon said: "There's a figure of a man for you! You could not kill him with a mallet. He almost knocked out the lintel, but little harm it did him."

And Matryona said: "Living as he does, how should he not grow strong? Death itself can't touch such a rock as that."

VII.

THEN SIMON SAID to Michael: "Well, we have taken the work, but we must see we don't get into trouble over it. The leather is dear, and the gentleman hot-tempered. We must make no mistakes. Come, your eye is truer and your hands have become nimbler than mine, so you take this measure and cut out the boots. I will finish off the sewing of the vamps."

Michael did as he was told. He took the leather, spread it out on the table, folded it in two, took a knife and began to cut out.

Matryona came and watched him cutting, and was surprised to see how he was doing it. Matryona was accustomed to seeing boots made, and she looked and saw that Michael was not cutting the leather for boots, but was cutting it round.

She wished to say something, but she thought to herself: "Perhaps I do not understand how gentleman's boots should be made. I suppose Michael knows more about it—and I won't interfere."

When Michael had cut up the leather, he took a thread and began to sew not with two ends, as boots are sewn, but with a single end, as for soft slippers.

Again Matryona wondered, but again she did not interfere. Michael sewed on steadily till noon. Then Simon rose for dinner, looked around, and saw that Michael had made slippers out of the gentleman's leather.

"Ah," groaned Simon, and he thought, "How is it that Michael, who has been with me a whole year and never made a mistake before, should do such a dreadful thing? The gentleman ordered high boots, welted, with whole fronts, and Michael has made soft slippers with single soles, and has wasted the leather. What am I to say to the gentleman? I can never replace leather such as this."

And he said to Michael, "What are you doing, friend? You have ruined me! You know the gentleman ordered high boots, but see what you have made!"

Hardly had he begun to rebuke Michael, when "rat-tat" went the iron ring that hung at the door. Someone was knocking. They looked out of the window; a man had come on horseback, and was fastening his horse. They opened the door, and the servant who had been with the gentleman came in.

"Good day," said he.

"Good day," replied Simon. "What can we do for you?"

"My mistress has sent me about the boots."

"What about the boots?"

"Why, my master no longer needs them. He is dead."

"Is it possible?"

"He did not live to get home after leaving you, but died in the carriage. When we reached home and the servants came to help him alight, he rolled over like a sack. He was dead already, and so stiff that he could hardly be got out of the carriage. My mistress sent me here, saying: 'Tell the bootmaker that the gentleman who ordered boots of him and left the leather for them no longer needs the boots, but that he must quickly make soft slippers for the corpse. Wait till they are ready, and bring them back with you.' That is why I have come."

Michael gathered up the remnants of the leather; rolled them up, took the soft slippers he had made, slapped them together, wiped them down with his apron, and handed them and the roll of leather to the servant, who took them and said: "Good-bye, masters, and good day to you!"

VIII.

ANOTHER YEAR PASSED, and another, and Michael was now living his sixth year with Simon. He lived as before. He went nowhere, only spoke when necessary, and had only smiled twice in all those years— once when Matryona gave him food, and a second time when the gentleman was in their hut. Simon was more than pleased with his workman. He never now asked him where he came from, and only feared lest Michael should go away.

They were all at home one day. Matryona was putting iron pots in the oven; the children were running along the benches and looking out of the window; Simon was sewing at one window, and Michael was fastening on a heel at the other.

One of the boys ran along the bench to Michael, leant on his shoulder, and looked out of the window.

"Look, Uncle Michael! There is a lady with little girls! She seems to be coming here. And one of the girls is lame."

When the boy said that, Michael dropped his work, turned to the window, and looked out into the street.

Simon was surprised. Michael never used to look out into the street, but now he pressed against the window, staring at something. Simon also looked out, and saw that a well-dressed woman was really coming to his hut, leading by the hand two little girls in fur coats and woolen shawls. The girls could hardly be told one from the other, except that one of them was crippled in her left leg and walked with a limp.

The woman stepped into the porch and entered the passage. Feeling about for the entrance she found the latch, which she lifted, and opened the door. She let the two girls go in first, and followed them into the hut.

"Good day, good folk!"

"Pray come in," said Simon. "What can we do for you?"

The woman sat down by the table. The two little girls pressed close to her knees, afraid of the people in the hut.

"I want leather shoes made for these two little girls for spring."

"We can do that. We never have made such small shoes, but we can make them; either welted or turnover shoes, linen lined. My man, Michael, is a master at the work."

Simon glanced at Michael and saw that he had left his work and was sitting with his eyes fixed on the little girls. Simon was surprised. It was true the girls were pretty, with black eyes, plump, and rosy-cheeked, and they wore nice kerchiefs and fur coats, but still Simon could not understand why Michael should look at them like that—just as if he had known them before. He was puzzled, but went on talking with the woman, and arranging the price. Having fixed it, he prepared the measure. The woman lifted the lame girl on to her lap and said: "Take two measures from this little girl. Make one shoe for the lame foot and three for the sound one. They both have the same size feet. They are twins."

Simon took the measure and, speaking of the lame girl, said: "How did it happen to her? She is such a pretty girl. Was she born so?"

"No, her mother crushed her leg."

Then Matryona joined in. She wondered who this woman was, and whose children were, so she said: "Are not you their mother then?"

"No, my good woman; I am neither their mother nor any relation to them. They were quite strangers to me, but I adopted them."

"They are not your children and yet you are so fond of them?"

"How can I help being fond of them? I fed them both at my own breasts. I had a child of my own, but God took him. I was not so fond of him as I now am of them."

"Then whose children are they?"

IX.

THE WOMAN, HAVING begun talking, told them the whole story.

"It is about six years since their parents died, both in one week: their father was buried on the Tuesday, and their mother died on the Friday. These orphans were born three days after their father's death, and their mother did not live another day. My husband and I were then living as peasants in the village. We were neighbors of theirs, our yard being next to theirs. Their father was a lonely man; a wood-cutter in the forest. When felling trees one day, they let one fall on him. It fell across his body and crushed his bowels out. They hardly got him home before his soul went to God; and that same week his wife gave birth to twins—these little girls. She was poor and alone; she had no one, young or old, with her. Alone she gave them birth, and alone she met her death."

"The next morning I went to see her, but when I entered the hut, she, poor thing, was already stark and cold. In dying she had rolled on to this child and crushed her leg. The village folk came to the hut, washed the body, laid her out, made a coffin, and buried her. They were good folk. The babies were left alone. What was to be done with them? I was the only woman there who had a baby at the time. I was nursing my first-born— eight weeks old. So I took them for a time. The peasants came together, and thought and thought what to do with them; and at last they said to me: 'For the present, Mary, you had better keep the girls, and later on we will arrange what to do for them.' So I nursed the sound one at my breast, but at first I did not feed this crippled one. I did not suppose she would live. But then I thought to myself, why should the poor innocent suffer? I pitied her, and began to feed her. And so I fed my own boy and these two—the three of them—at my own breast. I was young and strong, and had good food, and God gave me so much milk that at times it even overflowed. I used sometimes to feed two at a time, while the third was waiting. When one had enough I nursed the third. And God so ordered it that these grew up, while my own was buried before he was two years old. And I had no more children, though we prospered. Now my husband is working for the corn merchant at the mill. The pay is good, and we are well off. But I have no children of my own, and how lonely I should be without these little girls! How can I help loving them! They are the joy of my life!"

She pressed the lame little girl to her with one hand, while with the other she wiped the tears from her cheeks.

And Matryona sighed, and said: "The proverb is true that says, 'One may live without father or mother, but one cannot live without God.'"

So they talked together, when suddenly the whole hut was lighted up as though by summer lightning from the corner where Michael sat. They all looked towards him and saw him sitting, his hands folded on his knees, gazing upwards and smiling.

X.

THE WOMAN WENT away with the girls. Michael rose from the bench, put down his work, and took off his apron. Then, bowing low to Simon and his wife, he said: "Farewell, masters. God has forgiven me. I ask your forgiveness, too, for anything done amiss."

And they saw that a light shone from Michael. And Simon rose, bowed down to Michael, and said: "I see, Michael, that you are no common man, and I can neither keep you nor question you. Only tell me this: how is it that when I found you and brought you home, you were gloomy, and when my wife gave you food you smiled at her and became brighter? Then when the gentleman came to order the boots, you smiled again and became brighter still? And now, when this woman brought the little girls, you smiled a third time, and have become as bright as day? Tell me, Michael, why does your face shine so, and why did you smile those three times?"

And Michael answered: "Light shines from me because I have been punished, but now God has pardoned me. And I smiled three times, because God sent me to learn three truths, and I have learnt them. One I learnt when your wife pitied me, and that is why I smiled the first time. The second I learnt when the rich man ordered the boots, and then I smiled again. And now, when I saw those little girls, I learn the third and last truth, and I smiled the third time."

And Simon said, "Tell me, Michael, what did God punish you for? and what were the three truths? that I, too, may know them."

And Michael answered: "God punished me for disobeying Him. I was an angel in heaven and disobeyed God. God sent me to fetch a woman's soul. I flew to earth, and saw a sick woman lying alone, who had just given birth to twin girls. They moved feebly at their mother's side, but she could not lift them to her breast. When she saw me, she understood that God had sent me for her soul, and she wept and said: 'Angel of God! My husband has just been buried, killed by a falling tree. I have neither sister, nor aunt, nor mother: no one to care for my orphans. Do not take my soul! Let me nurse my babes, feed them, and set them on their feet before I die. Children cannot live without father or mother.' And I hearkened to her. I placed one child at her breast and gave the other into her arms, and returned to the Lord in heaven. I flew to the Lord, and said: 'I could not take the soul of the mother. Her husband was killed by a tree; the woman has twins, and prays that her soul may not be taken. She says: "Let me nurse and feed my children, and set them on their feet. Children cannot live without father or mother." I have not taken her soul.' And God said: 'Go—take the mother's soul, and learn three truths: Learn What dwells in man, What is not given to man, and What men live by. When thou has learnt these things, thou shalt return to heaven.' So I flew again to earth and took the mother's soul. The babes dropped from her breasts. Her body rolled over on the bed and crushed one babe, twisting its leg. I rose above the village, wishing to take her soul to God; but a wind seized me, and my wings drooped and dropped off. Her soul rose alone to God, while I fell to earth by the roadside."

XI.

AND SIMON AND Matryona understood who it was that had lived with them, and whom they had clothed and fed. And they wept with awe and with joy. And the angel said: "I was alone in the field, naked. I had never known human needs, cold and hunger, till I became a man. I was famished, frozen, and did not know what to do. I saw, near the field I was in, a shrine built for God, and I went to it hoping to find shelter. But the shrine was locked, and I could not enter. So I sat down behind the shrine to shelter myself at least from the wind. Evening drew on. I was hungry, frozen, and in pain. Suddenly I heard a man coming along the road. He carried a pair of boots, and was talking to himself. For the first time since I became a man I saw the mortal face of a man, and his face seemed terrible to me and I turned from it. And I heard the man talking to himself of how to cover his body from the cold in winter, and how to feed wife and children. And I thought: 'I am perishing of cold and hunger, and here is a man thinking only of how to clothe himself and his wife, and how to get bread for themselves. He cannot help me.' When the man saw me he frowned and became still more terrible, and passed me by on the other side. I despaired; but suddenly I heard him coming back. I looked up, and did not recognize the same man; before, I had seen death in his face; but now he was alive, and I recognized in him the presence of God. He came up to me, clothed me, took me with him, and brought me to his home. I entered the house; a woman came to meet us and began to speak. The woman was still more terrible than the man had been; the spirit of death came from her mouth; I could not breathe for the stench of death that spread around her. She wished to drive me out into the cold, and I knew that if she did so she would die. Suddenly her husband spoke to her of God, and the woman changed at once. And when she brought me food and looked at me, I glanced at her and saw that death no longer dwelt in her; she had become alive, and in her, too, I saw God.

"Then I remembered the first lesson God had set me: 'Learn what dwells in man.' And I understood that in man dwells Love! I was glad that God had already begun to show me what He had promised, and I smiled for the first time. But I had not yet learnt all. I did not yet know What is not given to man, and What men live by.

"I lived with you, and a year passed. A man came to order boots that should wear for a year without losing shape or cracking. I looked at him, and suddenly, behind his shoulder, I saw my comrade—the angel of death. None but me saw that angel; but I knew him, and knew that before the sun set he would take that rich man's soul. And I thought to myself, 'The man is making preparations for a year, and does not know that he will die before evening.' And I remembered God's second saying, 'Learn what is not given to man.'

"What dwells in man I already knew. Now I learnt what is not given him. It is not given to man to know his own needs. And I smiled for the second time. I was glad to have seen my comrade angel—glad also that God had revealed to me the second saying.

"But I still did not know all. I did not know What men live by. And I lived on, waiting till God should reveal to me the last lesson. In the sixth year came the girl-twins with the woman; and I recognized the girls, and heard how they had been kept alive. Having heard the story, I thought, 'Their mother besought me for the children's sake, and I believed her when she said that children cannot live without father or mother; but a stranger has nursed them, and has brought them up.' And when the woman showed her love for the children that were not her own, and wept over them, I saw in her the living God and understood What men live by. And I knew that God had revealed to me the last lesson, and had forgiven my sin. And then I smiled for the third time."

XII.

AND THE ANGEL'S body was bared, and he was clothed in light so that eye could not look on him; and his voice grew louder, as though it came not from him but from heaven above. And the angel said:

"I have learnt that all men live not by care for themselves but by love.

"It was not given to the mother to know what her children needed for their life. Nor was it given to the rich man to know what he himself needed. Nor is it given to any man to know whether, when evening comes, he will need boots for his body or slippers for his corpse.

"I remained alive when I was a man, not by care of myself, but because love was present in a passer-by, and because he and his wife pitied and loved me. The orphans remained alive not because of their mother's care, but because there was love in the heart of a woman, a stranger to them, who pitied and loved them. And all men live not by the thought they spend on their own welfare, but because love exists in man.

"I knew before that God gave life to men and desires that they should live; now I understood more than that.

"I understood that God does not wish men to live apart, and therefore he does not reveal to them what each one needs for himself; but he wishes them to live united, and therefore reveals to each of them what is necessary for all.

"I have now understood that though it seems to men that they live by care for themselves, in truth it is love alone by which they live. He who has love, is in God, and God is in him, for God is love."

And the angel sang praise to God, so that the hut trembled at his voice. The roof opened, and a column of fire rose from earth to heaven. Simon and his wife and children fell to the ground. Wings appeared upon the angel's shoulders, and he rose into the heavens.

And when Simon came to himself the hut stood as before, and there was no one in it but his own family.

(1881)
Translated by Aylmer Maude

Tolstoy adapted *"Где Любовь, Там и Бог,"* about a grief-stricken shoemaker transformed and enlightened by his daily readings of the New Testament, from an anonymous story translated into Russian as *"Uncle Martin."* After Tolstoy published his sophisticated and affecting version, the French author R. Saillens declared his authorship of the original. Excepting Saillens's plot, the tale is thoroughly Tolstoy's, who, by artistic reflex, creates a living, vividly imaginable man as well as the personages who enter Martýn Avdyéich's shop.

Beyond the immediacy of Tolstoy's characterizations, there are glorious artistic touches throughout the seemingly simple story, including a momentary change of point of view that illuminates the people and their situations: *"The woman was surprised. She saw an old man in an apron, with glasses over his nose, calling to her. She followed him in."* Tolstoy also dramatizes the act of reading with particular brilliance: *"When Avdyéich read these words, there was joy in his heart. He took off his glasses, put them on the book, leaned his arms on the table, and fell to musing."*

3

Where Love Is, There God Is Also

SHOEMAKER MARTÝN AVDYÉICH lived in the city. He lived in a basement, in a room with one window. The window looked out on the street. Through it the people could be seen as they passed by: though only the feet were visible, Martýn Avdyéich could tell the men by their boots. He had lived for a long time in one place and had many acquaintances. It was a rare pair of boots in the neighborhood that had not gone once or twice through his hands. Some he had resoled; on others he had put patches, or fixed the seams, or even put on new uppers. Frequently he saw his own work through the window. He had much to do, for he did honest work, put in strong material, took no more than was fair, and kept his word. If he could get a piece of work done by a certain time he undertook to do it, and if not, he would not cheat, but said so in advance. Everybody knew Avdyéich, and his work never stopped.

Avdyéich had always been a good man, but in his old age he thought more of his soul and came near unto God. Even while Martýn had been living with a master, his wife had died, and he had been left with a boy three years of age. Their children did not live long. All the elder children had died before. At first Martýn had intended sending his son to his sister in a village, but then he felt sorry for the little lad, and thought: "It will be hard for my Kapitóshka to grow up in somebody else's family, and so I will keep him."

Avdyéich left his master, and took up quarters with his son. But God did not grant Avdyéich any luck with his children. No sooner had the boy grown up so as to be a help to his father and a joy to him, than a disease fell upon him and he lay down and had a fever for a week and died. Martýn buried his son, and was in despair. He despaired so much that he began to murmur against God. He was so downhearted that more than once he asked God to let him die, and rebuked God for having taken his beloved only son, and not him. He even stopped going to church.

One day an old man, a countryman of Avdyéich's, returning from Tróitsa,—he had been a pilgrim for eight years,—came to see him. Avdyéich talked with him and began to complain of his sorrow: "I have even no desire to live any longer, godly man. If I could only die. That is all I am praying God for. I am a man without any hope."

And the old man said to him: "You do not say well, Martýn. We cannot judge God's works. Not by our reason, but by God's judgment do we live. God has determined that your son should die, and you live. Evidently it is better so. The reason you are in despair is that you want to live for your own enjoyment."

"What else shall we live for?" asked Martýn.

And the old man said: "We must live for God, Martýn. He gives us life, and for Him must we live. When you shall live for Him and shall not worry about anything, life will be lighter for you."

Martýn was silent, and he said: "How shall we live for God?"

And the old man said: "Christ has shown us how to live for God. Do you know how to read? If so, buy yourself a Gospel and read it, and you will learn from it how to live for God. It tells all about it."

These words fell deep into Avdyéich's heart. And he went that very day and bought himself a New Testament in large letters, and began to read.

Avdyéich had meant to read it on holidays only, but when he began to read it, his heart was so rejoiced that he read it every day. Many a time he buried himself so much in reading that all the kerosene would be spent in the lamp, but he could not tear himself away from the book. And Avdyéich read in it every evening, and the more he read, the clearer it became to him what God wanted of him, and how he should live for God; and his heart grew lighter and lighter. Formerly, when he lay down to sleep, he used to groan and sob and think of his Kapitóshka, but now he only muttered: "Glory be to Thee, glory to Thee, O Lord! Thy will be done!"

Since then Avdyéich's life had been changed. Formerly, he used on a holiday to frequent the tavern, to drink tea, and would not decline a drink of vódka. He would drink a glass with an acquaintance and, though he would not be drunk, he would come out of the tavern in a happier mood, and then he would speak foolish things, and would scold, or slander a man. Now all that passed away from him. His life came to be calm and happy. In the morning he sat down to work, and when he got through, he took the lamp from the hook, put it down on the table, fetched the book from the shelf, opened it, and began to read it. And the more he read, the better he understood it, and his mind was clearer and his heart lighter.

One evening Martýn read late into the night. He had before him the Gospel of St. Luke. He read the sixth chapter and the verses: "And unto him that smiteth thee on the one cheek offer also the other; and him that taketh away thy cloke forbid not to take thy coat also. Give to every man that asketh of thee; and of him that taketh away thy goods ask them not again. And as ye would that men should do to you, do ye also to them likewise."[8]

And he read also the other verses, where the Lord says: "And why call ye me, Lord, Lord, and do not the things which I say? Whosoever cometh to me, and heareth my sayings, and doeth them, I will shew you to whom he is like: he is like a man which built an house, and digged deep, and laid the foundation on a rock: and when the flood arose, the stream beat vehemently upon that house, and could not shake it: for it was founded upon a rock. But he that heareth, and doeth not, is like a man that without a foundation built an house

---

[8] Wiener quotes throughout from the King James Version of the Bible.

upon the earth; against which the stream did beat vehemently, and immediately it fell; and the ruin of that house was great."

When Avdyéich read these words, there was joy in his heart. He took off his glasses, put them on the book, leaned his arms on the table, and fell to musing. And he began to apply these words to his life, and he thought: "Is my house on a rock, or on the sand? It is well if it is founded on a rock: it is so easy to sit alone,—it seems to me that I am doing everything which God has commanded; but if I dissipate, I shall sin again. I will just proceed as at present. It is so nice! Help me, God!"

This he thought, and he wanted to go to sleep, but he was loath to tear himself away from the book. And he began to read the seventh chapter. He read about the centurion, about the widow's son, about the answer to John's disciples, and he reached the passage where the rich Pharisee invited the Lord to be his guest, and where the sinning woman anointed His feet and washed them with her tears, and he justified her. And he reached the 44th verse, and read: "And he turned to the woman, and said unto Simon, Seest thou this woman? I entered into thine house, thou gavest me no water for my feet: but she hath washed my feet with tears, and wiped them with the hairs of her head. Thou gavest me no kiss: but this woman since the time I came in hath not ceased to kiss my feet. My head with oil thou didst not anoint: but this woman hath anointed my feet with ointment."

When he had read these verses, he thought: "He gave no water for His feet; he gave no kiss; he did not anoint His head with oil."

And again Avdyéich took off his glasses and placed them on the book, and fell to musing.

"Evidently he was just such a Pharisee as I am. He, no doubt, thought only of himself: how to drink tea, and be warm, and in comfort, but he did not think of the guest. About himself he thought, but no care did he have for the guest. And who was the guest?—The Lord Himself. Would I have done so, if He had come to me?"

And Avdyéich leaned his head on both his arms and did not notice how he fell asleep.

"Martýn!" suddenly something seemed to breathe over his very ear.

Martýn shuddered in his sleep: "Who is that?"

He turned around and looked at the door, but there was nobody there. He bent down again, to go to sleep. Suddenly he heard distinctly: "Martýn, oh, Martýn, remember, tomorrow I will come to the street."

Martýn awoke, rose from his chair, and began to rub his eyes. He did not know himself whether he had heard these words in his dream or in waking. He put out the light and went to sleep.

Avdyéich got up in the morning before daybreak, said his prayers, made a fire, put the beet soup and porridge on the stove, started the samovár, tied on his apron, and sat down at the window to work. And, as he sat there at work, he kept thinking of what had happened the night before. His thoughts were divided: now he thought that it had only seemed so to him, and now again he thought he had actually heard the voice.

"Well," he thought, "such things happen."

Martýn was sitting at the window and not so much working as looking out into the street, and if somebody passed in unfamiliar boots, he bent over to look out of the window, in order to see not merely the boots, but also the face. A janitor passed by in new felt boots; then a water-carrier went past; then an old soldier of the days of Nicholas, in patched old felt boots, holding a shovel in his hands, came in a line with the window. Avdyéich recognized him by his felt boots. The old man's name was Stepánych, and he was living with a neighboring merchant for charity's sake. It was his duty to help the janitor. Stepánych began to clear away the snow opposite Avdyéich's window. Avdyéich cast a glance at him and went back to his work.

"Evidently I am losing my senses in my old age," Avdyéich laughed to himself. "Stepánych is clearing away the snow, and I thought that Christ was coming to see me. I, old fool, am losing my senses." But before he had made a dozen stitches, something drew him again toward the window. He looked out, and there he saw Stepánych leaning his shovel against the wall and either warming or resting himself.

He was an old, broken-down man, and evidently shoveling snow was above his strength. Avdyéich thought: "I ought to give him some tea; fortunately the samovár is just boiling." He stuck the awl into the wood, got up, placed the samovár on the table, put some tea in the teapot, and tapped with his finger at the window. Stepánych turned around and walked over to the window. Avdyéich beckoned to him and went to open the door.

"Come in and get warmed up!" he said. "I suppose you are feeling cold."

"Christ save you! I have a breaking in my bones," said Stepánych.

He came in, shook off the snow and wiped his boots so as not to track the floor, but he was tottering all the time.

"Don't take the trouble to rub your boots. I will clean up,—that is my business. Come and sit down!" said Avdyéich. "Here, drink a glass of tea!"

Avdyéich filled two glasses and moved one of them up to his guest, and himself poured his glass into the saucer and began to blow at it.

Stepánych drank his glass; then he turned it upside down, put the lump of sugar on top of it, and began to express his thanks; but it was evident that he wanted another glass.

"Have some more," said Avdyéich; and he poured out a glass for his guest and one for himself. Avdyéich drank his tea, but something kept drawing his attention to the window.

"Are you waiting for anybody?" asked the guest.

"Am I waiting for anybody? It is really a shame to say for whom I am waiting: no, I am not exactly waiting, but a certain word has fallen deep into my heart: I do not know myself whether it is a vision, or what. You see, my friend, I read the Gospel yesterday about Father Christ and how He suffered and walked the earth. I suppose you have heard of it?"

"Yes, I have," replied Stepánych, "but we are ignorant people,— we do not know how to read."

"Well, so I read about how He walked the earth. I read, you know, about how He came to the Pharisee, and the Pharisee did not give Him a good reception. Well, my friend, as I was reading last night about that very thing, I wondered how he could have failed to honor Father Christ. If He should have happened to come to me, for example, I should have done everything to receive Him. But he did not receive Him well. As I was thinking of it, I fell asleep. And as I dozed off I heard someone calling me by name: I got up and it was as though somebody were whispering to me: 'Wait,' he said: 'I will come tomorrow.' This he repeated twice. Would you believe it,— it has been running through my head,—I blame myself for it,—and I am, as it were, waiting for Father Christ."

Stepánych shook his head and said nothing. He finished his glass and put it sidewise, but Avdyéich took it again and filled it with tea.

"Drink, and may it do you good! I suppose when He, the Father, walked the earth, He did not neglect anybody, and kept the company mostly of simple folk. He visited mostly simple folk, and chose His disciples mostly from people of our class, laboring men, like ourselves the sinners. He who raises himself up, He said, shall be humbled, and he who humbles himself shall be raised. You call me Lord, He said, but I will wash your feet. He who wants to be the first, He said, let him be everybody's servant; because, He said, blessed are the poor, the meek the humble, and the merciful."

Stepánych forgot his tea. He was an old man and easily moved to tears. He sat there and listened, and tears flowed down his cheeks.

"Take another glass!" said Avdyéich.

But Stepánych made the sign of the cross, thanked him for the tea, pushed the glass away from him, and got up.

"Thank you, Martýn Avdyéich," he said. "You were hospitable to me, and have given food to my body and my soul."

"You are welcome. Come in again,—I shall be glad to see you," said Avdyéich.

Stepánych went away. Martýn poured out the last tea, finished another glass, put away the dishes, and again sat down at the window to work,—to tap a boot. And as he worked, he kept looking out of the window,—waiting for Christ and thinking of Him and His works. And all kinds of Christ's speeches ran through his head.

There passed by two soldiers, one in Crown boots, the other in boots of his own; then the proprietor of a neighboring house came by in clean galoshes, and then a baker with a basket. All of these went past the window, and then a woman in woolen stockings and peasant shoes came in line with the window. She went by the window and stopped near a wall. Avdyéich looked at her through the window, and saw that she was a strange, poorly dressed woman, with a child: she had stopped with her back to the wind and was trying to wrap the child, though she did not have anything to wrap it in. The woman's clothes were for the summer, and scanty at that. Avdyéich could hear the child cry in the street, and her vain attempt to quiet it. Avdyéich got up and went out of his room and up to the staircase, and called out: "Dear woman! Dear woman!"

The woman heard him and turned around.

"Why are you standing there in the cold with the child? Come in here! It will be easier for you to wrap the child in a warm room. Here, this way!"

The woman was surprised. She saw an old man in an apron, with glasses over his nose, calling to her. She followed him in.

They went down the stairs and entered the room, and Martýn took the woman up to the bed.

"Sit down here, clever woman, nearer to the stove, and get warm and feed the child."

"There is no milk in my breasts,—I have not had anything to eat since morning," said the woman, but still she took the child to her breast.

Avdyéich shook his head, went to the table, fetched some bread and a bowl, opened a door in the stove, filled the bowl with beet soup, and took out the pot of porridge, but it was not done yet. He put the soup on the table, put down the bread, and took off a rag from a hook and put it down on the table.

"Sit down, clever woman, and eat, and I will sit with the babe,—I used to have children of my own, and so I know how to take care of them."

The woman made the sign of the cross, sat down at the table, and began to eat, while Avdyéich seated himself on the bed with the child. He smacked his lips at it, but could not smack well, for he had no teeth. The babe kept crying all the time. Avdyéich tried to frighten it with his finger: he quickly carried his finger down toward the babe's mouth and pulled it away again. He did not put his finger into the child's mouth, because it was black,—all smeared with pitch. But the child took a fancy for his finger and grew quiet, and then began even to smile. Avdyéich, too, was happy. The woman was eating in the meantime and telling him who she was and whither she was going.

"I am a soldier's wife," she said. "My husband was driven some-where far away eight months ago, and I do not know where he is. I had been working as a cook when the baby was born; they would not keep me with the child. This is the third month that I have been without a place. I have spent all I had saved. I wanted to hire out as a wet-nurse, but they will not take me: they say that I am too thin. I went to a merchant woman, where our granny lives, and she promised she would take me. I thought she wanted me to come at once, but she told me she wanted me next week. She lives a distance away. I am all worn out and have worn out the dear child, too. Luckily our landlady pities us for the sake of Christ, or else I do not know how we should have lived until now."

Avdyéich heaved a sigh, and said: "And have you no warm clothes?"

"Indeed, it is time now to have warm clothing, dear man! But yesterday I pawned my last kerchief for twenty kopeks."

The woman went up to the bed and took her child, but Avdyéich got up, went to the wall, rummaged there awhile, and brought her an old sleeveless cloak.

"Take this!" he said. "It is an old piece, but you may use it to wrap yourself in."

The woman looked at the cloak and at the old man, and took the cloak, and burst out weeping. Avdyéich turned his face away; he crawled under the bed, pulled out a box, rummaged through it, and again sat down opposite the woman.

And the woman said: "May Christ save you, grandfather! Evidently He sent me to your window. My child would have frozen to death. When I went out it was warm, but now it has turned dreadfully cold. It was He, our Father, who taught you to look through the window and have pity on me, sorrowful woman."

Avdyéich smiled, and said: "It is He who has instructed me: clever woman, there was good reason why I looked through the window."

Martýn told the soldier woman about his dream, and how he had heard a voice promising him that the Lord would come to see him on that day.

"Everything is possible," said the woman. She got up, threw the cloak over her, wrapped the child in it, and began to bow to Avdyéich and to thank him.

"Accept this, for the sake of Christ," said Avdyéich, giving her twenty kopeks, with which to redeem her kerchief.

The woman made the sign of the cross, and so did Avdyéich, and he saw the woman out.

She went away. Avdyéich ate some soup, put the things away, and sat down once more to work. He was working, but at the same time thinking of the window: whenever it grew dark there, he looked up to see who was passing. There went by acquaintances and strangers, and there was nothing peculiar.

Suddenly Avdyéich saw an old woman, a huckstress, stop opposite the very window. She was carrying a basket with apples. There were but few of them left,—evidently she had sold all, and over her shoulder she carried a bag with woodchips. No doubt, she had picked them up at some new building, and was on her way home. The bag was evidently pulling hard on her shoulder; she wanted to shift it to her other shoulder, so she let the bag down on the flagstones, set the apple-basket on a post, and began to shake down the woodchips. While she was doing that, a boy in a torn cap leaped out from somewhere, grasped an apple from the basket, and wanted to skip out, but the old woman saw him in time and turned around and grabbed the boy by the sleeve. The boy yanked and tried to get away, but the old woman held on to him with both her hands, knocked down his cap, and took hold of his hair. The boy cried, and the old woman scolded. Avdyéich did not have time to put away the awl. He threw it on the floor, jumped out of the room, stumbled on the staircase, and dropped his glasses. He ran out into the street. The old woman was pulling the boy's hair and scolding him. She wanted to take him to a policeman; the little fellow struggled and tried to deny what he had done:

"I did not take any, so why do you beat me? Let me go!"

Avdyéich tried to separate them. He took the boy's arm, and said: "Let him go, granny, forgive him for Christ's sake!"

"I will forgive him in such a way that he will not forget until the new bath brooms are ripe. I will take the rascal to the police station!"

Avdyéich began to beg the old woman: "Let him go, granny, he will not do it again. Let him go, for Christ's sake!"

The woman let go of him. The boy wanted to run, but Avdyéich held on to him.

"Beg the grandmother's forgiveness," he said. "Don't do that again,—I saw you take the apple."

The boy began to cry, and he asked her forgiveness.

"That's right. And now, take this apple!" Avdyéich took an apple from the basket and gave it to the boy. "I will pay for it, granny," he said to the old woman.

"You are spoiling these ragamuffins," said the old woman. "He ought to be rewarded in such a way that he should remember it for a week."

"Oh, granny, granny!" said Avdyéich. "That is according to our ways, but how is that according to God's ways? If he is to be whipped for an apple, what ought to be done with us for our sins?"

The old woman grew silent.

And Avdyéich told the old woman the parable of the lord who forgave his servant his whole large debt, after which the servant went and took his fellow servant who was his debtor by the throat. The old woman listened to him, and the boy stood and listened, too.

"God has commanded that we should forgive," said Avdyéich, "or else we, too, shall not be forgiven. All are to be forgiven, but most of all an unthinking person."

The old woman shook her head and sighed.

"That is so," said the old woman, "but they are very much spoiled nowadays."

"Then we old people ought to teach them," said Avdyéich.

"That is what I say," said the old woman. "I myself had seven of them,—but only one daughter is left now." And the old woman began to tell where and how she was living with her daughter, and how many grandchildren she had. "My strength is waning," she said, "but still I work. I am sorry for my grandchildren, and they are such nice children,—nobody else meets me the way they do. Aksyútka will not go to anybody from me. 'Granny, granny dear, darling!'" And the old woman melted with tenderness.

"Of course, he is but a child,—God be with him!" the old woman said about the boy.

She wanted to lift the bag on her shoulders, when the boy jumped up to her, and said: "Let me carry it, granny! I am going that way."

The old woman shook her head and threw the bag on the boy's shoulders. They walked together down the street. The old woman had forgotten to ask Avdyéich to pay her for the apple. Avdyéich stood awhile, looking at them and hearing them talk as they walked along.

When they disappeared from sight, he returned to his room. He found his glasses on the staircase,—they were not broken,—and he picked up his awl and again sat down to work. He worked for awhile; he could not find the holes with the bristle, when he looked up and saw the lampman lighting the lamps.

"It is evidently time to strike a light," he thought, and he got up and fixed the lamp and hung it on the hook, and sat down again to work. He finished a boot: he turned it around and looked at it, and he saw that it was well done. He put down his tool, swept up the clippings, put away the bristles and the remnants and the awls, took the lamp and put it on the table, and fetched the Gospel from the shelf. He wanted to open the book where he had marked it the day before with a morocco clipping, but he opened it in another place. And just as he went to open the Gospel, he thought of his dream of the night before. And just as he thought of it, it appeared to him as though something were moving and stepping behind him. He looked around, and, indeed, it looked as though people were standing in the dark corner, but he could not make out who they were. And a voice whispered to him:

"Martýn, oh, Martýn, have you not recognized me?"

"Whom?" asked Avdyéich.

"Me," said the voice. "It is I."

And out of the dark corner came Stepánych, and he smiled and vanished like a cloud and was no more.

"And it is I," said a voice.

And out of the dark corner came the woman with the babe, and the woman smiled and the child laughed, and they, too, disappeared.

"And it is I," said a voice.

And out came the old woman and the boy with the apple, and both smiled and vanished.

And joy fell on Avdyéich's heart, and he made the sign of the cross, put on his glasses, and began to read the Gospel, there where he had opened it. And at the top of the page he read: "I was an hungered, and ye gave me meat: I was thirsty, and ye gave me drink: I was a stranger, and ye took me in."

And at the bottom of the page he read: "Inasmuch as ye have done it unto one of the least of these my brethren, ye have done it unto me." (Matthew, xxv.)

And Avdyéich understood that his dream had not deceived him, that the Savior had really come to him on that day, and that he had received Him.

(1885)
Translated by Leo Wiener

Tolstoy delighted in learning stories from the wandering storyteller Vasily Petrovich Shchegolenok. Among them, besides "What Men Live By," was this, "Три Старца," which scenario Tolstoy also probably knew from an 1859 book of Russian folk tales. "The Three Hermits" is a relatively rare example of Tolstoy's sense of humor while also a characteristic display of his appreciation for simplicity and directness over formality. The teacher, in this case a bishop of the Russian Orthodox Church, learns humility from his divinely humble students: "The Bishop sat down on a stone, and the old men stood before him, watching his mouth, and repeating the words as he uttered them. And all day long the Bishop labored, saying a word twenty, thirty, a hundred times over, and the old men repeated it after him. They blundered, and he corrected them, and made them begin again."

4

The Three Hermits
An Old Legend Current in the Volga District

"And in praying use not vain repetitions, as the Gentiles do: for they think that they shall be heard for their much speaking. Be not therefore like unto them: for your Father knoweth what things ye have need of, before ye ask Him."—Matthew, vi. 7, 8.[9]

A BISHOP WAS sailing from Archangel to the Solovétsk Monastery; and on the same vessel were a number of pilgrims on their way to visit the shrines at that place. The voyage was a smooth one. The

---

[9] Aylmer Maude lightly adapts the King James Version of the Bible.

wind favorable, and the weather fair. The pilgrims lay on deck, eating, or sat in groups talking to one another. The Bishop, too, came on deck, and as he was pacing up and down, he noticed a group of men standing near the prow and listening to a fisherman, who was pointing to the sea and telling them something. The Bishop stopped, and looked in the direction in which the man was pointing. He could see nothing, however, but the sea glistening in the sunshine. He drew nearer to listen, but when the man saw him, he took off his cap and was silent. The rest of the people also took off their caps, and bowed.

"Do not let me disturb you, friends," said the Bishop. "I came to hear what this good man was saying."

"The fisherman was telling us about the hermits," replied one, a tradesman, rather bolder than the rest.

"What hermits?" asked the Bishop, going to the side of the vessel and seating himself on a box. "Tell me about them. I should like to hear. What were you pointing at?"

"Why, that little island you can just see over there," answered the man, pointing to a spot ahead and a little to the right. "That is the island where the hermits live for the salvation of their souls."

"Where is the island?" asked the Bishop. "I see nothing."

"There, in the distance, if you will please look along my hand. Do you see that little cloud? Below it, and a bit to the left, there is just a faint streak. That is the island."

The Bishop looked carefully, but his unaccustomed eyes could make out nothing but the water shimmering in the sun.

"I cannot see it," he said. "But who are the hermits that live there?"

"They are holy men," answered the fisherman. "I had long heard tell of them, but never chanced to see them myself till the year before last."

And the fisherman related how once, when he was out fishing, he had been stranded at night upon that island, not knowing where he was. In the morning, as he wandered about the island, he came across an earth hut, and met an old man standing near it. Presently two others came out, and after having fed him, and dried his things, they helped him mend his boat.

"And what are they like?" asked the Bishop.

"One is a small man and his back is bent. He wears a priest's cassock and is very old; he must be more than a hundred, I should say. He is so old that the white of his beard is taking a greenish tinge, but he is always smiling, and his face is as bright as an angel's from heaven. The second is taller, but he also is very old. He wears a tattered, peasant coat. His beard is broad, and of a yellowish gray color. He is a strong man. Before I had time to help him, he turned my boat over as if it were only a pail. He too, is kindly and cheerful. The third is tall, and has a beard as white as snow and reaching to his knees. He is stern, with over-hanging eyebrows; and he wears nothing but a mat tied round his waist."

"And did they speak to you?" asked the Bishop.

"For the most part they did everything in silence, and spoke but little even to one another. One of them would just give a glance, and the others would understand him. I asked the tallest whether they had lived there long. He frowned, and muttered something as if he were angry; but the oldest one took his hand and smiled, and then the tall one was quiet. The oldest one only said: "Have mercy upon us," and smiled."

While the fisherman was talking, the ship had drawn nearer to the island.

"There, now you can see it plainly, if your Grace will please to look," said the tradesman, pointing with his hand.

The Bishop looked, and now he really saw a dark streak—which was the island. Having looked at it a while, he left the prow of the vessel, and going to the stern, asked the helmsman: "What island is that?"

"That one," replied the man, "has no name. There are many such in this sea."

"Is it true that there are hermits who live there for the salvation of their souls?"

"So it is said, your Grace, but I don't know if it's true. Fishermen say they have seen them; but of course they may only be spinning yarns."

"I should like to land on the island and see these men," said the Bishop. "How could I manage it?"

"The ship cannot get close to the island," replied the helmsman, "but you might be rowed there in a boat. You had better speak to the captain."

The captain was sent for and came.

"I should like to see these hermits," said the Bishop. "Could I not be rowed ashore?"

The captain tried to dissuade him.

"Of course it could be done," said he, "but we should lose much time. And if I might venture to say so to your Grace, the old men are not worth your pains. I have heard say that they are foolish old fellows, who understand nothing, and never speak a word, any more than the fish in the sea."

"I wish to see them," said the Bishop, "and I will pay you for your trouble and loss of time. Please let me have a boat."

There was no help for it; so the order was given. The sailors trimmed the sails, the steersman put up the helm, and the ship's course was set for the island. A chair was placed at the prow for the Bishop, and he sat there, looking ahead. The passengers all collected at the prow, and gazed at the island. Those who had the sharpest eyes could presently make out the rocks on it, and then a mud hut was seen. At last one man saw the hermits themselves. The captain brought a telescope and, after looking through it, handed it to the Bishop.

"It's right enough. There are three men standing on the shore. There, a little to the right of that big rock."

The Bishop took the telescope, got it into position, and he saw the three men: a tall one, a shorter one, and one very small and bent, standing on the shore and holding each other by the hand.

The captain turned to the Bishop.

"The vessel can get no nearer in than this, your Grace. If you wish to go ashore, we must ask you to go in the boat, while we anchor here."

The cable was quickly let out, the anchor cast, and the sails furled. There was a jerk, and the vessel shook. Then a boat having been lowered, the oarsmen jumped in, and the Bishop descended the ladder and took his seat. The men pulled at their oars, and the boat moved rapidly towards the island. When they came within a stone's throw, they saw three old men: a tall one with only a mat tied round his waist: a shorter one in a tattered peasant coat, and a very old one bent with age and wearing an old cassock—all three standing hand in hand.

The oarsmen pulled in to the shore, and held on with the boathook while the Bishop got out.

The old men bowed to him, and he gave them his benediction, at which they bowed still lower. Then the Bishop began to speak to them.

"I have heard," he said, "that you, godly men, live here saving your own souls, and praying to our Lord Christ for your fellow men. I, an unworthy servant of Christ, am called, by God's mercy, to keep and teach His flock. I wished to see you, servants of God, and to do what I can to teach you, also."

The old men looked at each other smiling, but remained silent.

"Tell me," said the Bishop, "what you are doing to save your souls, and how you serve God on this island."

The second hermit sighed, and looked at the oldest, the very ancient one. The latter smiled, and said: "We do not know how to serve God. We only serve and support ourselves, servant of God."

"But how do you pray to God?" asked the Bishop.

"We pray in this way," replied the hermit. "Three are ye, three are we, have mercy upon us."

And when the old man said this, all three raised their eyes to heaven, and repeated: "Three are ye, three are we, have mercy upon us!"

The Bishop smiled.

"You have evidently heard something about the Holy Trinity," said he. "But you do not pray aright. You have won my affection, godly men. I see you wish to please the Lord, but you do not know how to serve Him. That is not the way to pray; but listen to me, and I will teach you. I will teach you, not a way of my own, but the way in which God in the Holy Scriptures has commanded all men to pray to Him."

And the Bishop began explaining to the hermits how God had revealed Himself to men; telling them of God the Father, and God the Son, and God the Holy Ghost.

"God the Son came down on earth," said he, "to save men, and this is how He taught us all to pray. Listen, and repeat after me: 'Our Father.'"

And the first old man repeated after him, "Our Father," and the second said, "Our Father," and the third said, "Our Father."

"Which art in heaven," continued the Bishop.

The first hermit repeated, "Which art in heaven," but the second blundered over the words, and the tall hermit could not say them properly. His hair had grown over his mouth so that he could not speak plainly. The very old hermit, having no teeth, also mumbled indistinctly.

The Bishop repeated the words again, and the old men repeated them after him. The Bishop sat down on a stone, and the old men stood before him, watching his mouth, and repeating the words as he uttered them. And all day long the Bishop labored, saying a word twenty, thirty, a hundred times over, and the old men repeated it after him. They blundered, and he corrected them, and made them begin again.

The Bishop did not leave off till he had taught them the whole of the Lord's prayer so that they could not only repeat it after him, but could say it by themselves. The middle one was the first to know it, and to repeat the whole of it alone. The Bishop made him say it again and again, and at last the others could say it too.

It was getting dark, and the moon was appearing over the water, before the Bishop rose to return to the vessel. When he took leave of the old men, they all bowed down to the ground before him. He raised them, and kissed each of them, telling them to pray as he had taught them. Then he got into the boat and returned to the ship.

And as he sat in the boat and was rowed to the ship he could hear the three voices of the hermits loudly repeating the Lord's prayer. As the boat drew near the vessel their voices could no longer be heard, but they could still be seen in the moonlight, standing as he had left them on the shore, the shortest in the middle, the tallest on the right, the middle one on the left. As soon as the Bishop had reached the vessel and got on board, the anchor was weighed and the sails unfurled. The wind filled them, and the ship sailed away, and the Bishop took a seat in the stern and watched the island they had left. For a time he could still see the hermits, but presently they disappeared from sight, though the island was still visible. At last it too vanished, and only the sea was to be seen, rippling in the moonlight.

The pilgrims lay down to sleep, and all was quiet on deck. The Bishop did not wish to sleep, but sat alone at the stern, gazing at the sea where the island was no longer visible, and thinking of the good old men. He thought how pleased they had been to learn the Lord's prayer; and he thanked God for having sent him to teach and help such godly men.

So the Bishop sat, thinking, and gazing at the sea where the island had disappeared. And the moonlight flickered before his eyes, sparkling, now here, now there, upon the waves. Suddenly he saw something white and shining, on the bright path which the moon cast across the sea. Was it a seagull, or the little gleaming sail of some small boat? The Bishop fixed his eyes on it, wondering.

"It must be a boat sailing after us," thought he, "but it is overtaking us very rapidly. It was far, far away a minute ago, but now it is much nearer. It cannot be a boat, for I can see no sail; but whatever it may be, it is following us, and catching us up."

And he could not make out what it was. Not a boat, nor a bird, nor a fish! It was too large for a man, and besides a man could not be out there in the midst of the sea. The Bishop rose, and said to the helmsman: "Look there, what is that, my friend? What is it?" the Bishop repeated, though he could now see plainly what it was—the three hermits running upon the water, all gleaming white, their grey beards shining, and approaching the ship as quickly as though it were not moving.

The steersman looked and let go the helm in terror.

"Oh Lord! The hermits are running after us on the water as though it were dry land!"

The passengers hearing him, jumped up, and crowded to the stern. They saw the hermits coming along hand in hand, and the two outer ones beckoning the ship to stop. All three were gliding along upon the water without moving their feet. Before the ship could be stopped, the hermits had reached it, and raising their heads, all three as with one voice, began to say: "We have forgotten your teaching, servant of God. As long as we kept repeating it we remembered, but when we stopped saying it for a time, a word dropped out, and now it has all gone to pieces. We can remember nothing of it. Teach us again."

The Bishop crossed himself, and leaning over the ship's side, said: "Your own prayer will reach the Lord, men of God. It is not for me to teach you. Pray for us sinners."

And the Bishop bowed low before the old men; and they turned and went back across the sea. And a light shone until daybreak on the spot where they were lost to sight.

(1886)
Translated by Aylmer Maude

"Божеское и Человеческое" was conceived by Tolstoy in 1897 as part of his novel about the Russian justice and penal system, Resurrection *(1899), but he detached it amid revision of the novel and developed it as its own short story in 1904 and 1905. He published it in his 1906 anthology of inspirational and reflective stories,* Circle of Reading.

Tolstoy based two of the protagonists on revolutionaries of the late 1870s and 1880s. Anatoly Svetlogub is an idealistic, handsome, privileged, young man beloved for his generosity, sincerity, and kindliness. While in prison and awaiting his execution, he is given a New Testament; he reads and "the further he read, the more and more often he came to the thought that in this book something especially important was being said [...] such as he had never heard before but had been, as it were, long familiar to him." In contrast, there is the fearsome Ignaty Mezhenetsky, "whom everyone regarded as a person of unwavering will-power and unconquerable logic, completely devoted to the revolutionary cause." Mezhenetsky might seem to some to anticipate the future leader of the Bolshevik Revolution, Vladimir Lenin. The Old Believer, meanwhile, anonymous in the story, was based on an Old Believer who had visited Tolstoy's home at Yasnaya Polyana. (Old Believers were adherents of the old Russian church rituals; despite persecution, they continued to resist the Patriarch Nikon's reformation of the Orthodox Church, which occurred in the middle of the seventeenth century.)

5

Divine and Human

I.

IT WAS IN the '70s in Russia, at the very height of the revolutionaries' fight with the government.

The governor-general of the Southern Region was sitting behind his desk in his office one evening; he was a hardy German with a droopy mustache, a cold look and an inexpressive face; his military coat had a white cross on the neck. There were four candles in green shades on the table, and he was reviewing and signing papers that had been left for him by a ministry official. "Adjutant-General Such-and-Such," he signed each off with a long flourish, and set it aside.

Among the papers was a verdict for a death sentence by hanging of a Novorossiya University student, Anatoly Svetlogub, for his part in a conspiracy that had the goal of overthrowing the present government. Frowning deeply, the general signed off on this one too. His pale, well-groomed fingers, wrinkled with age and soap, neatly lined up the edges of the sheets and placed them to the side. The next paper concerned the allocation of monies for transporting provisions. He carefully read this paper, wondering whether it was a true accounting, when suddenly he was reminded of a conversation with his assistant about the matter concerning Svetlogub. The general held that finding the dynamite at Svetlogub's could not prove his criminal intent. His assistant, however, urged that besides the dynamite, there was ample evidence proving that Svetlogub had been the leader of the gang. Remembering this, the general gave it pause, but under his coat, with its wadding on the chest and lapels stiff as cardboard, his heart began to beat unevenly, and he started breathing so heavily that the big white cross, which was his pride and joy, began to stir on his chest. It was still possible to call back the ministry official and if not undo then postpone the verdict.

"Call him back? Or not call him back?"

His heart began to beat even more irregularly. He called. With a quick, noiseless step, the courier came in.

"Has Ivan Matveevich left?"

"Not at all, sir, your excellency; he was pleased to take himself to the chancellery."

The general's heart stopped, then beat rapidly. He remembered the warning of the doctor who had checked his heart the other day.

"The main thing," the doctor had said, "as soon as you feel that it's your heart, stop working, relax. The worst thing of all is agitation. Under no circumstances let it come to that."

"Are you ordering him summoned?"

"No, never mind," said the general. "Yes," he said to himself, "indecisiveness agitates worst of all. It's signed—and finished. As you've made your bed, you must sleep in it," he told himself, in his favorite German proverb. "And this doesn't concern me. I'm an executor of the supreme will, and I have to stand above such considerations," he added, knitting his eyebrows in order to bring out in himself the cruelty that was not in his heart.

And then he was reminded of his most recent meeting with the emperor, as the emperor, making a severe face and fixing his glassy gaze on him, said, "I'm relying on you: as you didn't spare yourself in the war, so you will be as resolute in the fight with the Reds—you won't let them fool or frighten you. Farewell!" And the emperor, embracing him, offered him his shoulder to be kissed. The general remembered this and how he had answered the emperor: "I have only one desire—to give my life to the service of my emperor and fatherland."

Recalling the feeling of obsequious tenderness that he had derived from the consciousness of his selfless loyalty to the emperor, he drove off the momentarily confusing thought, signed the remaining papers, and rang once more.

"The tea has been served?" he asked.

"It's being served now, your excellency."

"Fine; go now."

The general sighed deeply, and rubbing his hand over the spot where his heart was, he walked with a heavy step into the big, empty hall and across the hall's freshly polished parquet into the drawing room, from which voices carried.

The general's wife had guests: the governor and his wife; an old princess, who was a great patriot; and a Guards officer, the fiancé of the general's last unmarried daughter.

The general's dried-up wife, who had a cold face and thin lips, was sitting at a low little table, on which stood a tea set with a silver teapot on a heated ring. In an artificially sad tone she was telling the governor's wife, a stout lady who put on youthful airs, about her worry over her husband's health.

"Every day there are more and more dispatches revealing conspiracies and all kinds of terrible things. ... And it all falls on Basil, he has to resolve it all."

"Oh, perish the thought!" said the princess, and continued in French: "I become furious when I think about that accursed breed."

"Yes, yes, it's horrible! Would you believe he works twelve hours a day—and with his weak heart. I am really afraid ..."

Having seen her husband come in, she did not continue.

"Yes, you must certainly hear him. Barbini—an amazing tenor," she said, smiling pleasantly at the governor's wife, meaning the newly arrived singer who had just arrived—as naturally as if they had been talking only about this.

The general's daughter, a sweet-looking, plump young woman, was sitting with her fiancé in the far corner of the drawing room behind some Chinese screens. She stood up and walked with her fiancé over to her father.

"Goodness, we haven't seen each other all day!" said the general, kissing his daughter and pressing her fiancé's hand.

Having greeted the guests, the general sat at the table and chatted with the governor about the latest news.

"No, no, it's forbidden to discuss business!" the general's wife interrupted the governor. "And here, by the way, is Kopev; he'll tell us something amusing. Greetings, Kopev."

And Kopev, a well-known cutup and wit, did tell the latest joke, which made everyone laugh.

II.

"But no, this can't be, it can't, it can't! Let me go!" Svetlogub's mother shrieked, tearing herself from the arms of the schoolteacher—a friend of her son's—and the doctor, who were trying to restrain her.

Svetlogub's mother was not old; she was a sweet-looking woman with graying curls and starlike wrinkles around her eyes. The teacher, Svetlogub's friend, having learned that the death sentence was signed, had wanted to carefully prepare her for the fearsome news, but as soon as he began speaking about her son, she guessed, by the tone of his voice, by the timidity of his gaze, that what she feared had happened.

This occurred in a small room of the city's best hotel.

"But why are you holding me, let me go!" she shouted, tearing herself away from the doctor, an old friend of the family, who with one hand held her by her skinny elbow; with his other hand, he placed a glass on the oval table in front of the sofa. She was glad they were holding her because she felt that she needed to do something—but what, she didn't know, and she was frightened of herself.

"Calm yourself. Here, take some valerian drops," said the doctor, giving her the glass of cloudy liquid.

She went suddenly quiet and bent almost double; she laid her head on her sunken chest, and, closing her eyes, slumped onto the sofa.

She remembered how her son, three months ago, had bidden her farewell with a mysterious and despondent face. Then she remembered the eight-year-old boy in the velvet jacket with his bare little legs and long curling locks of blond hair.

"And him, him, this very boy ... they're doing this to him."

She jumped up, pushed aside the table, and tore herself from the doctor's hands. Reaching the door, she fell back into an armchair.

"And they say God exists! What kind of God is it if he allows this! The Devil take him, that God!" she shouted, now sobbing, now shuddering with a hysterical laugh. "They're going to hang him, hang him, he who gave up everything, his whole career, he gave his entire fortune to others, to the people, he gave it all away," she said. Before, she had always reproached her son for this; now she was realizing to herself the merit of his self-renunciation. "And him, him, they're doing this to him! And you say there's a God!" she cried out.

"But I'm not saying anything, I'm only asking you to take the drops."

"I don't want anything. Ha-ha-ha!" she laughed and sobbed, wallowing in her despair.

By nighttime she was so exhausted that she could no longer speak or weep; she only gazed unmovingly before her with a fixed, crazed look. The doctor injected her with morphine, and she fell asleep.

Her sleep was dreamless, but her awakening was more horrible than before. Most horrible of all was that people could be so cruel, not only these horrible generals with shaven cheeks and the gendarmes, but everything, everyone: the servant-girl with the calm face coming in to clean the room, and the people in the next room, a cheerful gathering that was laughing about something as if none of this had happened.

III.

Svetlogub had spent two months in a solitary cell, during which time he had endured much.

From childhood, Svetlogub had unconsciously felt the falseness of his privileged situation as a rich person, and despite trying to suppress this consciousness, it often happened that when he encountered the people's need and sometimes simply when things were going especially well and happily for him, he became ashamed before those people—peasants, old folks, women, children—who were born, grew up and died, not only not knowing all those pleasures of which he partook nor valuing them, but never even escaping drudgery and need. When he graduated from the university, to free himself from the consciousness of his transgression, he set up in his village a school—a model elementary school, a cooperative store and a shelter for impoverished old men and old women. But, strange to say, when occupied with those matters he was far more ashamed in the presence of the people than when he dined with acquaintances or bought an expensive horse. He felt that all this was not right and, worse, that there was something bad in it, something morally dirty.

During one of those states of disappointment in his village activity, he went to Kiev and met with one of his closest university classmates. Three years after this meeting, this classmate was shot dead in the Kiev fortress's moat.

This classmate, an ardent, enthusiastic man of great gifts, led him to take part in a group whose aim was to enlighten the people, raising in them a consciousness of their rights and forming among them unified circles that strove for their liberation from the power of the landowners and government. It was as if conversations with this man and his friends brought to Svetlogub a clear consciousness of everything that until then he had felt hazily. He understood now what he needed to do. Not breaking off his contact with his new comrades, he left for the village and began a completely new activity. He became a teacher himself and started classes for grown-ups; he read them books and pamphlets, and explained to the peasants their situation; moreover, he printed illegal popular books and pamphlets, and gave away everything that he could—without depriving his mother—for the construction of such centers in other villages.

From the very first steps of this new activity, Svetlogub encountered two unexpected obstacles: one was that the majority of the common people were not only indifferent to his preachings but looked on him contemptuously. (Only the exceptional ones, often people of doubtful morals, understood him and sympathized with him.) Another obstacle was from the government side. He was barred from the school, and they searched his home and the homes of people close to him, and their books and papers were confiscated.

Svetlogub gave little attention to the first obstacle—the indifference of the people because he was too outraged by the second obstacle: the government oppression was senseless and insulting. His comrades experienced the same in their activity elsewhere, and the sense of irritation against the government that was mutually kindled in them all reached the point where most of this circle decided to fight the government with violence.

The head of this circle was one Mezhenetsky, whom everyone regarded as a person of unwavering will-power and unconquerable logic, completely devoted to the revolutionary cause.

Svetlogub submitted to the influence of this man; and with the same energy as when he had worked among the people, he now gave himself over to terrorist activity.

This activity was dangerous, but the very danger was what attracted Svetlogub most of all.

He said to himself: "Victory or martyrdom, but if it's martyrdom, then martyrdom is a victory, but only in the future." The fire lit in him was not only not extinguished in the next seven years of his revolutionary activity but burned higher and higher, supported as he was by the love and respect of the people among whom he circulated.

He attributed no importance to the fact that he had given away almost all of his fortune—the fortune passed down to him from his father—for this cause, nor to the difficulties and need that he often bore in this activity. Only one thing distressed him: this was the grief his activity caused his mother and the young woman, her ward, who lived with his mother and who loved him.

Recently an unpleasant comrade for whom he had no liking, a terrorist wanted by the police, asked him to hide dynamite in his home. Without hesitation, Svetlogub agreed, mostly because he didn't like this comrade, and the next day a search was made of Svetlogub's apartment and the dynamite was found. To all the questions about how and from whom he had received the dynamite, Svetlogub refused to give an answer.

And the martyrdom that he had expected began for him. Lately, when so many of his friends had been executed, imprisoned, or exiled, and when so many women suffered, Svetlogub had almost desired martyrdom. In the first minutes of his arrest and questioning, he felt a certain excitement, almost joy.

He experienced this feeling when they stripped him and searched him, and when they brought him into the prison and locked the iron door behind him. But when a day passed, another, a third, when a week passed, another, a third, in the dirty, damp cell full of insects, and in solitary confinement and involuntary idleness, interrupted only by knockings on the wall with fellow prisoners, who passed along nothing but bad and joyless news, and occasional questionings by cold, hostile people trying to extract from him accusations of comrades, his moral strength, along with his physical vigor, steadily weakened, and he only yearned for and desired, as he told himself, some end to this tormenting situation. His yearning was increased by his doubts as to his own strength. During the second month of his imprisonment, he found himself thinking that he would tell the whole truth, just to be released. He was horrified by his weakness, but he couldn't find within himself his former strength, and he hated and despised himself and yearned even more.

The most horrible thing was that in his imprisonment, he began to miss the youthful strength and joys that he had so lightly sacrificed while at liberty and now seemed to him so charming that he regretted what he had considered good, sometimes regretted all his activity. Thoughts came to him about how happily and well he could have lived in freedom—in the village, at liberty, abroad, among his favorite and loving friends. He could marry her or maybe another, and live a simple, joyful, radiant life with her.

IV.

ON ONE OF the tormentingly uniform days of imprisonment, in the second month, the warden on his usual rounds gave Svetlogub a little book with a gold cross on the brown cover, saying that the governor's wife had visited the prison and left copies of the Gospels, which were permitted to be given to the prisoners. Svetlogub thanked him and gave a slight smile, setting the book on a small table that was bolted to the wall.

When the warden left, Svetlogub talked with his neighbor by tapping, telling him that the warden had been and said nothing new, but only brought him the Gospels, and his neighbor answered that it had been the same with him.

After lunch Svetlogub opened the book, its pages stuck together from dampness, and began reading. Svetlogub had never before read the Gospels as a book. Everything that he knew about it was what the religious teacher in his schooldays had passed along or what the priests and deacons had chanted in church.

"Chapter One. The book of the generation of Jesus Christ, the son of David, the son of Abraham. Abraham begat Isaac; and Isaac begat Jacob; and Jacob begat Judas ..."[10] he read. "Zorobabel begat

---

[10] The translations of the quotations from the Bible are from the King James Version (1611). It is most probable that the Old Believer was using a "people's version," the Synodal translation of the New Testament (that differed from the Russian Orthodox Church's), first published in Russia in 1822. (See https://www.readyrussian.org/Handouts/Grammar%2025--Russian%20Synodal%20Bible.html.)

Abiud," he continued reading. This was all as he expected: some kind of confusing, entirely unnecessary nonsense. If he hadn't been in prison, he would not have been able to finish a single page, but here he continued reading just to be reading. "Like Gogol's Petrushka," he thought to himself.[11] He read through the first chapter about the virgin birth and about the prophecy that the one begotten would be called Emmanuel, meaning "God is with us." "And where's the prophecy in this?" he thought, and continued reading. He read through the second chapter about the wandering star, and the third chapter about John who ate locusts, and the fourth about a devil proposing that Christ perform the gymnastic exercise of jumping off a roof.

All this seemed so uninteresting to him that, despite the tedium of prison, he already wanted to close the book and begin his usual evening occupation of taking off his shirt and catching the fleas he found there when suddenly he remembered that in the fifth year of school he had forgotten one of the Beatitudes, and the rosy-faced, curly-haired priest suddenly got angry and gave him a two out of five. He could not remember which Beatitude this was and read them all. "Blessed are they which are persecuted for righteousness' sake: for theirs is the kingdom of heaven," he read. "This, it seems, concerns us too," he thought. "Blessed are ye, when men shall revile you, and persecute you, and shall say all manner of evil against you falsely, for my sake. Rejoice, and be exceeding glad: for great is your reward in heaven: for so persecuted they the prophets which were before you. Ye are the salt of the earth: but if the salt have lost his savor, wherewith shall it be salted? It is thenceforth good for nothing, but to be cast out, and to be trodden under foot of men."

"This certainly applies to us," he thought, and continued reading further. Having read the whole fifth chapter, he fell to musing: "Don't get angry, don't commit adultery, suffer evil, love your enemies."

"Yes, if everyone lived that way," he thought, "there would be no need for revolution." Reading further, he went more and more deeply into the meaning of those places of the book that were fully comprehensible. And the further he read, the more and more often he came to the thought that in this book something especially important was being said. It was important and simple and touching, such as he had never heard before but had been, as it were, long familiar to him.

---

[11] This refers to Chichikov's sidekick Petrushka in Nikolay Gogol's *Dead Souls*: "Not the words which he read, but the mere solace derived from the act of reading, was what especially pleased his mind [...]" (translated by C. J. Hogarth).

"Then said Jesus unto his disciples, If any man will come after me, let him deny himself, and take up his cross, and follow me. For whosoever will save his life shall lose it: and whosoever will lose his life for my sake shall find it. For what is a man profited, if he shall gain the whole world, and lose his own soul? or what shall a man give in exchange for his soul?"

"Yes, yes, that's just it!" he suddenly cried out with tears in his eyes. "That's just what I wanted to do. Yes, I wanted just this: to give away my soul; not to keep it but to give it away. In this there is joy, in this is life. I did a lot for people, for human glory," he thought. "Not for glory from the crowd, but for the glory of the kind opinion of those whom I valued and loved: Natasha, Dmitriy Shelomov—and then there were the doubts, there was the anxiety. It was good for me only when I did things that my soul demanded, when I wanted to give away myself, to give all of myself away…"

From that day on, Svetlogub began spending the bulk of his time reading and pondering what was said in this book. This reading roused in him not only a state of tenderness that took him out of the conditions in which he found himself; it also roused such cogitation as he had never before been conscious of in himself. He wondered why people, all people, did not live as was said in this book. "Because living so is good not for one alone but for all. Only live so, and there will be no sorrow, no need; there will be only bliss. If only this would end, if only I might be free again," he sometimes thought. "Someday they will let me out, or send me to hard labor. It's all the same, it's possible to live so anywhere. I will live so. It is possible and necessary to live so; not to live so is madness."

V.

ON ONE OF those days when he found himself in a joyful, excited state like that, the warden came into his cell at an unusual time and asked if he was well and whether he desired anything. Svetlogub was startled, not understanding what this change meant, and asked for cigarettes, expecting a refusal. But the warden said that he would send for some right away; and a guard did bring him a pack of cigarettes and some matches.

"Someone must have petitioned for me," thought Svetlogub, and, having lit up a cigarette, began walking back and forth in the cell, thinking over the meaning of this change.

The next day they brought him to court. In the courtroom, where he had already been several times, they did not start questioning him. Instead, one of the judges, not looking at him, stood up from his chair, and the others stood up too; and that judge, holding a paper in his hands, began reading in a loud, unnaturally inexpressive voice.

Svetlogub listened and looked at the judges' faces. Not one of them was looking at him, but all of them were listening with meaningfully gloomy faces.

On the paper it said that Anatoly Svetlogub, for his proven part in revolutionary activity having the goal in the nearer or more distant future of overthrowing the present government, was sentenced to the deprivation of all rights and to death by hanging.

Svetlogub listened and understood the meaning of the words pronounced by the presiding judge. He noticed the absurdity of "in the near or distant future" of overthrowing the present government and the deprivation of personal rights of one sentenced to death, but he absolutely did not understand the meaning for himself of what had been read out.

Only long after they had told him that he could go, and he had gone outside with the gendarme, did he begin to understand what had been announced to him.

"There's something wrong here, wrong … It's some sort of nonsense. This can't be," he said to himself as he sat in the carriage that was taking him back to the prison.

He felt in himself such a force of life that he was unable to imagine death: he could not unite the consciousness of "I" with death, with the absence of "I."

Having returned to prison, Svetlogub sat on the cot and, closing his eyes, tried to vividly imagine what awaited him, and he couldn't do it at all. He could not at all imagine that he would not be or that people could wish to kill him.

"Me, a young, kind, happy man, beloved by so many people," he thought. He remembered the love that his mother, Natasha, and his friends had for him. "They're going to kill me, hang me! Who would do this, and why? And then, what will there be when I am no more? It can't be," he said to himself.

The warden came. Svetlogub hadn't heard him enter.

"Who's this? Why are you here?" said Svetlogub, not recognizing the warden. "Oh yes, it's you! When is this to be?" he asked.

"That's not for me to know," said the warden, and having stood silently for several seconds, he suddenly, with an ingratiatingly gentle voice, said, "Our priest here would like to … accomp—… he would like to see you …"

"I don't need it, don't need it, I don't need anything! Go away!" Svetlogub cried out.

"Oughtn't you to write to someone? That's possible," said the warden.

"Yes, yes, send the things. I'll write."

The warden left.

"In the morning, then" thought Svetlogub. "They always do it like that. Tomorrow morning I will no longer be … No, it can't be, it's a dream."

But the guard came in, the regular, familiar guard, and he brought two pens, an inkwell, a packet of postal paper and bluish envelopes, and drew the stool up to the table. All this was real and not a dream.

"It's necessary not to think, not think. Yes, yes, write. I'll write to Mama," thought Svetlogub, sitting down on the stool and beginning to write.

"My sweet one, my dear one," he wrote and burst into tears. "Forgive me, forgive me for all the sorrow that I have caused you. Whether I was mistaken or not, I could not have done otherwise. I ask for one thing: forgive me."—"But I already wrote that," he thought. "Well, but it's all the same, there's no time to rewrite it now."—"Don't suffer over me," he wrote on. "A little earlier, a little later … isn't it all the same? I'm not afraid, and I don't regret what I did. I could not have done otherwise. Only forgive me. And don't be angry at them—neither at those with whom I worked, nor at those who are executing me. Neither could have done otherwise. Forgive them, for they know not what they do. About myself, I don't dare repeat those words, but they are in my soul, and they lift me and console me. Forgive me, I kiss your sweet, wrinkled old hands!" Two tears, one after the other, dripped onto the paper and spread across it. "I am weeping, though not from sorrow or fear, but from a tenderness in the face of the most solemn moment of my life and because I love you. Do not reproach my friends but love them. Especially Prokhorov, precisely because he was the reason for my death. It is so joyful to love not he who is guilty but he who could be reproached and hated. Loving such a person—an enemy—is such happiness. Tell Natasha that her love was my consolation and joy. I didn't understand this clearly, but in the depths of my soul I was conscious of it. Knowing that she existed and loved me, it was easier for me to live. Well, I've said everything. Farewell!"

He reread the letter and, towards the end, reading Prokhorov's name, he suddenly remembered that the letter might be scrutinized, probably would be scrutinized, and this would ruin Prokhorov.

"My God, what have I done!" he suddenly cried out and, tearing the letter into long strips, began carefully burning them in the lamp.

He had sat down to write in despair, but now he felt himself at peace, almost joyful.

He took up another sheet and immediately began writing. Thoughts, one after the other, crowded in his head.

"Sweet, darling Mama," he wrote, and again his eyes clouded over with tears, and he had to wipe them off with the sleeve of his prison robe to see what he was writing. "To what extent did I not know myself, not know the full strength of my love for you and the gratitude that always lived in my heart! Now I know and feel it, and when I remember our quarrels, the unkind words that I said to you, it pains me and shames me, and it's almost incomprehensible. Forgive me and remember only the good, if there was any in me.

"I'm not afraid of death. Truthfully speaking, I don't understand it, don't believe in it. For if there is death, annihilation, then isn't it all the same to die thirty years or thirty minutes earlier or later? And if there is no death, it's absolutely all the same, whether earlier or later."

"But why am I philosophizing?" he thought. "I need to say what was in that letter—something good at the end. Yes."

"Don't reproach my friends, but love them, especially he who was the unintentional reason for my death. Kiss Natasha for me and tell her that I loved her always."

He folded the letter, sealed it and sat on his bed, placing his hands on his knees and swallowing his tears.

He still did not believe that he had to die. Having again posed the question to himself several times as to whether he was dreaming, he tried in vain to wake up. And this thought brought him to another: about whether all life in this world wasn't a dream, the awakening from which would be death. "And if this is so, isn't the consciousness of life in this world only an awakening from a dream of a previous life, the details of which I don't remember? So that life here is not the beginning but only a new form of life. I'll die and pass into a new form." He liked this thought; but when he wanted to rely on it, he felt that neither this thought nor any thought, whatever it was, could render him fearless before death. Finally he wearied of thinking. His brain wouldn't work anymore. He closed his eyes and for a long time sat there like that, not thinking.

"So then? What will there be?" he remembered again. "Nothing? No, not nothing. But what then?"

And it suddenly became absolutely clear to him that for a living person there were not and could not be answers to these questions.

"So why then am I asking myself about this? Why? Yes, why? It's not necessary to ask, it's necessary to live, as I was living just now, when I was writing this letter. Because we were all sentenced a long time ago, forever, and yet we live. We live well, joyfully, when … we love. Yes, when we love. Here I was writing the letter, I was loving, and for me it was good. It's necessary to live like that. And it's possible to live everywhere and always, in freedom, in prison, and now, and tomorrow, and to the very end."

He wanted to speak fondly, lovingly, with someone then and there. He knocked on the door, and when the sentry looked in at him, he asked him what time it was and whether he would soon be relieved from duty, but the sentry gave him no answer at all. Then he asked him to call the warden. The warden came, asking what he needed.

"Here I've written a letter to my mother; give it to her, please," he said, and tears rose into his eyes at the memory of his mother.

The warden took the letter, promising to deliver it, and wanted to leave, but Svetlogub stopped him.

"Listen, you're a kind man. Why do you serve in this oppressive position?" he asked, touching him fondly on the sleeve.

The warden smiled with an unnatural ruefulness and, lowering his eyes, said: "A man has to live."

"But you could leave this position. Because you can always find employment. You're such a kind person. Maybe I could have …"

The warden suddenly sobbed, quickly turned, and left, slamming the door.

The warden's agitation made Svetlogub feel even more tender, and, holding back joyful tears, he began pacing from wall to wall, now experiencing no fear, only a state of tenderness that raised him above the world.

The very question of what would happen to him after death, which he had tried so hard to answer but could not, seemed decided for him, and not by any positive, rational answer but by his consciousness of the true life that was within him.

And he remembered the words of the Gospel: "Verily, verily, I say unto you, Except a corn of wheat fall into the ground and die, it abideth alone: but if it die, it bringeth forth much fruit."

"Here I am falling into the ground. Yes, verily, verily," he thought.

"Sleep now," he thought, all of a sudden. "So as not to be weak later." He lay on the cot, closed his eyes and fell right to sleep.

He woke at six in the morning, fully under the impression of a light, merry dream. He had dreamed that he and a little blonde girl were climbing spreading trees that were strewn with ripe black cherries, and they were gathering them in a big copper basin. But the cherries did not fall into the basin and spilled onto the ground, and some kind of strange creatures, somewhat catlike, caught the cherries and tossed them up and caught them again. And watching this, the girl broke into laughter; she laughed loud and so infectiously that Svetlogub also laughed merrily in his sleep, not knowing why. The copper basin suddenly slipped out of the girl's hands, and Svetlogub wanted to catch it, but he couldn't quite, and the basin, with a metallic clatter, bumping along the branches, fell onto the ground. And he woke up, smiling and still hearing the continuing clatter of the basin. This clatter was the sound of iron bolts opening in the corridor. Steps were heard in the corridor and the clanking of rifles. He suddenly remembered everything. "Oh, if I could only sleep again!" Svetlogub thought, but sleep was now impossible. The steps came to his door. He heard the key seeking the lock and the creaking of the door as it opened.

A gendarme officer, the warden and a convoy entered.

"Death? Well, so what? I'll go. Yes, this is good. All is good," thought Svetlogub, feeling the return of that solemnly tender state in which he had been the night before.

VI.

IN THE VERY prison where Svetlogub was held, they were also holding an Old Believer, a priestless one who doubted his leaders and was searching for the true faith. He denied not only the Nikonian church, but also the government from the time of Peter, the tsar whom he considered the anti-Christ. The tsarist authority he called "the tobacco power," and he bravely said what he thought, denouncing priests and officials, for which he was tried and held in a stockade and sent from one prison to another. That he was not at liberty but in prison, that the wardens cursed at him, that they shackled him, that he was mocked by fellow prisoners, that they all, just like the higher-ups, had renounced God, and they swore at one another and defiled in every way the divine image in themselves, all this did not interest him; he had seen all this everywhere in the world when he was at liberty. All this, he knew, proceeded from people having lost the true faith, and all had wandered off like blind puppies from their mother. Yet he knew that the true faith existed. He knew this because he felt this faith in his heart. And he looked for this faith everywhere. Most of all he hoped to find it in the Revelation of John.

"He that is unjust, let him be unjust still: and he which is filthy, let him be filthy still: and he that is righteous, let him be righteous still: and he that is holy, let him be holy still. And, behold, I come quickly; and my reward is with me, to give every man according as his work shall be." And he constantly read this mysterious book, and every moment awaited the one who would "come," who would not only give to each "according as his work shall be" but would reveal the whole divine truth to people.

On the morning of Svetlogub's execution, the Old Believer heard the drums and, climbing up to the window, saw through the bars the wagon being brought up and a young man with radiant eyes and curly locks leaving the prison, smiling as he stepped into the wagon. In the young man's small white hand was a book. The young man pressed the book to his heart—the Old Believer recognized that it was the Gospels—and he nodded at the prisoners in the windows, smiling and exchanging glances with them. The horses set out, and the wagon with the young man seated in it, radiant as an angel and surrounded by guards, went rumbling over the stones as it drove out through the gate.

The Old Believer climbed down from the window, sat on his cot and mused. "That one knew the truth," he thought. "Therefore the servants of the anti-Christ will choke him with a rope, so that he doesn't reveal it to anyone."

VII.

IT WAS AN overcast fall morning. The sun could not be seen. From the sea blew a warm, moist wind.

The fresh air, the sight of homes, the city, the horses, the people looking at him—all this distracted Svetlogub. Sitting on the wagon's bench, his back to the driver, he involuntarily looked into the faces of the convoy soldiers and at the locals they met on the way.

It was an early hour of the morning; the streets they took him through were almost empty, and they encountered only working people. The bricklayers in aprons, splattered with lime, walking hurriedly toward him, stopped and turned back when they caught up with the wagon. One of them said something and waved a hand, and they all turned and went back to their work; the carters hauling rattling iron bars turned their huge horses aside so as to make way for the wagon; they stopped and looked at him with uncomprehending curiosity. One of them took off his cap and crossed himself. A cook in a white apron and cap, with a basket in her hand, came out through some gates, but, seeing the wagon, quickly returned to the yard and ran back out with another woman, and both, with bated breath, followed the wagon with wide open eyes as long as they could see it. With energetic gestures, some gray-haired unshaven fellow in torn clothing was impressing something evidently disapproving on a yard-man, pointing at Svetlogub. Two boys came trotting up to the wagon and, with heads turned, not looking before them, walked on the sidewalk alongside it. One, the older, walked with quick steps; the other, small and not wearing a cap, was holding onto the older boy and looking fearfully at the wagon; on his short legs, he hurried, with difficulty and stumbling, after the older boy. Meeting his eyes, Svetlogub nodded at him. This gesture of the fearsome man being carried in a wagon so confused the boy that, with his eyes popping and his mouth agape, he was about to cry. Then Svetlogub, kissing his own hand, smiled fondly at him. And the boy suddenly, unexpectedly, answered with a sweet, kind smile.

During the whole journey, the consciousness of what awaited him did not disturb Svetlogub's peacefully solemn mood.

It was only when the wagon rolled up to the gallows, and he was led down from it and saw the posts with the crossbeam and the rope slightly swaying in the breeze, that he felt as if he had been physically struck in the heart. He suddenly felt sick to his stomach. But this didn't last long. Around the scaffold he saw dark rows of soldiers with rifles. Officers walked in front of the soldiers. And as soon as they had begun taking him out of the wagon, there resounded the unexpected crack of a drumroll that caused him to shudder. Behind the rows of soldiers, Svetlogub saw the carriages of the ladies and gentlemen who had evidently come to view the spectacle. At first, the sight of all this surprised Svetlogub, but as soon as he remembered how he had been before prison, he felt pity that these people didn't know what he now knew. "But they will find out. I will die, but the truth won't die. They will know. And how everyone—well, not I, but all of them—could be and will be happy."

They led him to the scaffold, and an officer walked behind him. The drums went silent, and an officer read out, in an unnatural voice that sounded especially faint after the clatter of the drums in the midst of the wide field, that stupid death sentence that had been read to him in court: about the deprivation of all rights for the one they were killing and about the nearer or more distant future. "Why, why are they doing all this?" thought Svetlogub. "What a pity that they still don't know and that I can no longer communicate everything to them, but they will know. Everyone will know."

A skinny priest with long sparse hair and wearing a purple cassock approached Svetlogub; he had a single, small gold cross on his chest and another cross that was big and silver, which he held in a weak, pale, veined, thin hand that extended from a black velvet cuff.

"Merciful Lord," he began, transferring the cross from his left hand to his right and holding it out to Svetlogub.

Svetlogub shuddered and drew back. He nearly said an unkind word to the priest who spoke of mercy while taking part in the deed that was being visited upon him, but, remembering the words of the Gospel, "They know not what they do," he made an effort and uttered shyly, "Forgive me, but this is not necessary for me. Please, forgive me, but for me it's truly not necessary! I thank you."

He extended his hand to the priest. The priest again transferred the cross into his left hand, and then, pressing Svetlogub's hand while trying not to look him in the face, he descended from the scaffold. The drums again cracked, drowning out all the other sounds. After the priest, a middle-aged man with sloping shoulders and muscular arms, wearing a jacket over a Russian blouse, came up to Svetlogub, his quick steps shaking the scaffold's planks. Quickly looking Svetlogub over, this person approached quite close to him, and, enveloping him in an unpleasant odor of wine and sweat, grabbed his arms with vice-like fingers above the wrists, squeezing them hard enough to hurt, bent them behind his back and tightly bound them. Having bound the arms, the executioner stopped momentarily, as if considering something, glancing now at Svetlogub, now at some things that he had brought with him and had set on the scaffold, now at the rope hanging on the crossbeam. Having considered what he needed to do, he approached the rope, did something with it, and moved Svetlogub forward, closer to the rope and the scaffold's sheer drop.

Just as happened at the announcement of the death sentence, when Svetlogub could not understand the full meaning of what was being announced to him, so now he could not take in the full significance of the present moment, and looked with surprise at the executioner, who was hurriedly, skillfully, and anxiously carrying out his horrible business. The executioner's face was that of a typical Russian worker's, not evil but concentrated, as happens with people who are trying to carry out as precisely as possible a necessary and complicated piece of work.

"Move over, you … or, no—kindly move over …" instructed the executioner in a hoarse voice, pushing him toward the gallows. Svetlogub moved over.

"Lord help me, have mercy on me!" he said.

Svetlogub did not believe in God and had often even laughed at people who believed in God. He did not believe in God now, did not believe because not only could he not express the idea of God in words, he also could not embrace it in thought. But what he now understood by the him to whom he was appealing—he knew it was more real than anything else he knew. He also knew that this appeal was necessary and important. He knew this because the appeal immediately consoled and strengthened him.

He moved toward the gallows and involuntarily surveyed the rows of soldiers and the motley spectators and once more wondered, "Why, why are they doing this?" And he felt pity for them and for himself, and tears came to his eyes.

"Don't you pity me?" he said, having caught a glance from the executioner's sharp gray eyes.

The executioner paused for a moment. His face suddenly grew evil.

"Oh, you! Chattering away!" he muttered, and quickly stooped to the floor, where his coat and a piece of canvas lay, and with a deft movement, grasped Svetlogub from behind with both hands; he drew a canvas bag over Svetlogub's head and hurriedly pulled it down to the middle of his back and chest.

"Into thy hands I commend my spirit,"[12] Svetlogub said, recalling the words of the Gospels.

His spirit did not oppose death, but his strong, young body did not accept it, did not submit and wanted to fight.

---

[12] From the King James Version of the Bible, Luke 23:46.

He wanted to scream, tear himself away, but at that moment he felt a tug, the loss of a foothold, an animal terror of suffocation, a noise in his head and then the disappearance of everything.

Svetlogub's body hung swinging on the rope. His shoulders raised and lowered twice.

Having waited a couple of minutes, the executioner, frowning grimly, placed his hands on the corpse's shoulders and with a strong motion pulled on it. All of the corpse's movements ceased, except for the slow swinging of a doll hanging in a sack with an unnaturally jutting head and legs stretched out in prison socks.

Coming down from the scaffold, the executioner reported to the supervisor that the corpse could be taken from the noose and buried.

An hour later, the corpse was taken from the gallows and carted off to an unconsecrated cemetery.

The executioner had carried out what he had wanted to and had taken upon himself to carry out. But carrying this out had not been easy. Svetlogub's words—"Don't you pity me?"—never left his head. He was a murderer and convict himself, and the calling of executioner had given him a relative freedom and luxury in life, but after this day he refused to further carry out the duty he had taken on, and in that same week he drank away not only the money he had received for the execution, but also all of his relatively expensive clothing, and it came to the point where he was put in a punishment cell, and from the punishment cell he was moved to a hospital.

VIII.

IGNATY MEZHENETSKY, ONE of the heads of the revolutionaries' terrorist party and the very one who had drawn Svetlogub into terrorist activity, was transferred from the region where they had arrested him to St. Petersburg. In that same prison was also confined the Old Believer who had seen Svetlogub's execution. They were sending him to Siberia. He was still constantly thinking about how and where he might learn what the true faith was, and he sometimes recalled the radiant young man who smiled joyfully on the way to his death.

Discovering that in this prison with him there was a comrade of that young man, a person at one with him in faith, the Old Believer rejoiced and asked the watchman to bring him to Svetlogub's friend.

Despite all the strictness of the prison discipline, Mezhenetsky had not stopped communicating with the people of his party and awaited news each day about the excavation that he had devised and invented in order to blow the tsar's train sky high. Now, remembering some overlooked details, he was considering the means by which to convey them to his fellow-thinkers. When the guard came to his cell and cautiously, quietly said to him that one of the prisoners wanted to see him, he was gladdened, hoping that this meeting would give him the opportunity to connect with his party.

"Who is he?" he asked.

"A peasant."

"What's he want?"

"He wants to talk about faith."

Mezhenetsky smiled. "Very well, send him," he said. "They, those Old Believers, also hate the government. Maybe he will prove useful," he thought.

The guard left and a few minutes later opened the door and let a dry, short old man into the cell; he had bushy hair, a sparse, gray goatee and kind, tired, light blue eyes.

"What do you want?" asked Mezhenetsky.

The old man peered up at him and, immediately lowering his eyes, put out a small, vigorous, dry hand.

"What do you want?" Mezhenetsky repeated.

"A word with you."

"What sort of word?"

"About faith."

"What faith?"

"They say you are of one faith with that young 'un that the servants of the anti-Christ choked with a rope in Odessa."

"What young man?"

"The one they choked in Odessa come autumn."

"Svetlogub, probably?"

"The very one. He was a friend to you?" With each question, the old man directed his kind eyes probingly into Mezhenetsky's face, and then right away lowered them again.

"Yes, he was a person close to me."

"And of one faith?"

"One, if you must," said Mezhenetsky smiling.

"It's about this, my word with you."

"What do you actually need?"

"To know your faith."

"Our faith ... Well, sit down," said Mezhenetsky, shrugging his shoulders. "Our faith lies in this. We believe that there are people who have seized power and now torment and deceive the people, and that it's necessary not to spare oneself but to fight those people in order to free from them the people, whom they exploit—" Mezhenetsky said by force of habit. "They torment," he corrected himself. "And so now it's necessary to annihilate them. They murder, and it's necessary to murder them until they come to their senses."

The old man sighed, not raising his eyes.

"Our faith is not to spare oneself, to overthrow the despotic government and establish one that is free, elective and popular."

The old man sighed heavily, stood up, adjusted the lapels of his prison robe, went down on his knees and lay at Mezhenetsky's feet, beating his forehead on the filthy floorboards.

"Why are you bowing?"

"Don't deceive me, reveal what your faith consists of," said the old man, not rising, and not lifting his head.

"I said where our faith lies. Stand up now, or I won't speak anymore."

The old man got up.

"Was that where the young man's faith lay?" he said, standing before Mezhenetsky and now and then looking him in the face with his kindly eyes and right away lowering them again.

"That it was, and for that they hanged him. And now for that same faith they're taking me to the Peter and Paul Fortress."

The old man bowed from his waist and silently left the cell.

"No, that was not where the young man's faith lay," he thought. "That young man knew the true faith, but this one was either boasting that he is one with him in faith or he doesn't want to reveal it. ... Still, I will not give up. Neither here nor in Siberia. God is everywhere, people are everywhere. To go where you are bound, you must inquire your way,"[13] thought the old man, and again picked up the New Testament, which opened of itself to Revelation and, putting on his glasses, he sat by the window and began reading it.

---

[13] The Old Believer seems to be quoting from the Russian translation of Shakespeare's *Coriolanus* (III: i). Tolstoy was working on a book about Shakespeare as he finished "Divine and Human."

IX.

SEVEN MORE YEARS went by. Mezhenetsky served his time in solitary confinement at the Peter and Paul Fortress and was transferred to hard labor.

He had endured much during those seven years, but the direction of his thoughts did not change, and his energy did not weaken. In the questioning before his confinement in the fortress, he surprised the investigators and judges with his firmness and contemptuous attitude toward the people in whose power he found himself. In the depths of his soul, he suffered that he had been caught and that he could not complete the work he had started, but he did not show this; as soon as he came into close contact with people, the energy of his anger rose in him. To the questions they posed to him, he was silent, and he spoke only when there was an opportunity to nettle his questioners—the gendarme officer or the prosecutor.

When they said to him the habitual phrase—"You can ease your situation with an honest confession"—he would smile contemptuously, and after a short silence, would say: "If you think a reward or fear will force me to betray my comrades, you're judging me by yourselves. Do you really think that when doing the deed for which you are condemning me, I did not ready myself for the worst? You cannot surprise me with anything; you can't frighten me. Do what you can to me, whatever you want, but I won't speak."

And it pleased him to see how they looked at one another in confusion.

When, at the Peter and Paul Fortress, they placed him in a small, damp cell with dark glass in the high window, he understood that this wasn't for months but for years—and horror descended on him. The well-appointed, deathly quiet was horrible, and his consciousness that he was not alone, but that here, within these impenetrable walls, were confined prisoners such as himself: sentenced for ten, for twenty years, being killed, being hanged, or going out of their minds, or slowly dying of consumption. There were women and men, and maybe friends ... "The years will go by, and you too will go out of your mind or hang yourself or die, and no one will find out about you," he thought.

And anger rose in his soul at all people, especially at those who were the cause of his imprisonment. This anger required the presence of objects for his anger, required movement, noise. But here was deathly quiet, the soft footsteps of silent ones who didn't answer questions from people, the sounds of unlocking and locking doors, food at the usual hours, visits from silent people, the light of the rising sun through the dingy glass, the darkness and that same quiet, those same soft footsteps, and the one and the same sounds. Such as they were now, so they would be tomorrow. ... And his anger, finding no outlet for itself, ate away at his heart.

He tried knocking, but nobody answered him, and his knocking only brought about again those same soft footsteps and the measured voice of a person threatening him with the punishment cell.

The only time of rest and relaxation was in sleep. But then the awakening was horrible. In dreams he always saw himself in freedom, and for the most part he was preoccupied with things that he considered at odds with revolutionary activity. He was either playing on a strange violin or chasing after young women or riding in a boat or being awarded a doctorate at a foreign university for having made some strange scientific discovery and delivering a grateful speech at a dinner. These dreams were so vivid while reality was so boring and monotonous that in his memory he hardly distinguished them from reality.

The only difficult thing in dreams was that he mostly awoke at the moment when what he had striven for, what he desired, was about to transpire. Suddenly there was a thump of his heart—and the whole joyful situation disappeared. There remained a tormenting, unsatisfied desire, and again he was surrounded by damp-streaked gray walls lit by a lamp and under his body, a hard straw mattress flattened down on one side.

Sleep was the best time. But the longer his imprisonment continued, the less he slept. He awaited sleep as the greatest happiness, he desired it, but the more he desired it, the more it wandered off. All he had to do was ask himself "Am I falling asleep?" and all his sleepiness wore away.

Running and jumping in his cage did not help. The increased movements only caused weakness and an even greater excitement of his nerves, and made the crown of his head ache. He had only to close his eyes and against a dark, spangled background there began to emerge ghastly faces—shaggy, bald, big-mouthed, wry-mouthed, each one more fearsome than the previous. The faces grimaced with the most horrible grimaces. Then the faces began appearing even when his eyes were open, not only faces but entire figures, and began speaking and dancing. It became fearsome; he would jump up, beat his head on the wall and shout. The little window in the door would open.

"No shouting," a calm, even voice would say.

"Send for the warden!" shouted Mezhenetsky. He received no answer, and the little window would close.

And such despair would seize Mezhenetsky that he desired only one thing—death.

One time, in such circumstances, he resolved to take his own life. In his cell was a vent on which it was possible to fasten a noosed rope so that, standing on the cot, he could hang himself. But there was no rope. He began tearing up his sheet into narrow strips, but there were too few of these strips. Then he decided to starve himself to death and did not eat for two days, but on the third day he weakened, and the fit of hallucinations repeated with especial strength. When they brought him his meal, he was lying unconscious on the ground with open eyes.

The doctor came, laid him on the cot, gave him a bromide and morphine, and he slept.

When he woke up the next day, the doctor was standing over him and shaking his head. And suddenly the invigorating anger familiar to him from before, which he hadn't experienced for a long time, seized Mezhenetsky.

"How are you not ashamed to work here!" he said to the doctor then, when the latter, inclining his head, was taking his pulse. "Why do you treat me in order to torture me again? Because it's like being present at a flogging and authorizing it to be repeated."

"I will trouble you to lie on your back," said the unperturbed doctor, not looking at him and taking an osculation instrument from his side pocket.

"They healed the wounds in order to finish the remaining five thousand strokes of the stick. To hell with you, to the devil with you!" he suddenly yelled, throwing his legs off the cot. "Get out, I'll croak without you!"

"That's not good, young man. We have our own ways of answering rudeness."

"To hell with you, to hell!"

And Mezhenetsky was so fearsome that the doctor hurried away.

X.

EITHER BECAUSE OF the medications he had taken or because he had survived the crisis or because the anger that had arisen against the doctor had cured him, from that time on, he took himself in hand and began another life.

"They can't and won't hold me here forever," he thought. "They will free me one day. Maybe, most likely, there will be a change of regime (our people will continue working), and so it's necessary to take care of my life in order to leave here strong and healthy, and be in a position to continue the work."

He long pondered the best way to live for this purpose, and came up with this: he lay down at nine o'clock and forced himself to lie there—sleeping or not sleeping, either way—until five in the morning. At five o'clock he would get up, tidy, wash, do gymnastics, and then, as he said to himself, run his errands. And in his imagination he walked around Petersburg, from Nevsky to Nadezhdinskaya, trying to imagine everything that might be met on this trek: signs, homes, police officers, the carriages and pedestrians that he encountered. On Nadezhdinskaya he entered the home of an acquaintance and colleague, and there they, together with other comrades who arrived later, discussed their upcoming enterprise. Arguments and debates arose. Mezhenetsky spoke both for himself and for the others. Sometimes he spoke aloud, so that the guard gave him a warning through the little window, but Mezhenetsky did not pay him any mind and continued his imaginary Petersburg day. Having spent two hours at the friend's, he returned home and dined, first in his imagination, and then in reality, on the meal they brought him; he always ate in moderation. Then he, in his imagination, sat at home and studied history, mathematics, and sometimes, on Sundays, literature. The study of history consisted in choosing an epoch and a people, recalling the facts and the chronology. The study of mathematics consisted in doing calculations and geometry in his head. (He especially loved this study.) On Sundays he recalled Pushkin, Gogol, and Shakespeare, and composed works himself.

Before sleep, he made one more little excursion in his imagination, conducting with his comrades, both men and women, joking, merry, and occasionally serious discussions, sometimes ones from before, sometimes newly contrived. This went on until nightfall. Before sleep, for exercise, he took two thousand actual steps in his cage, and lay down on his cot and more often than not fell asleep.

The next day was just the same. Sometimes he traveled to the south and exhorted the people, started a rebellion and, together with the people, drove off the landowners and divided up the land among the peasants. All this, however, he imagined to himself not all at once but gradually, with all the details. In his imagination, his revolutionary party always triumphed everywhere, the government power weakened and had to convene a council. The tsar's family and all the oppressors of the people disappeared, and a republic was established, and he, Mezhenetsky, was elected president. Sometimes he got to this point too quickly, and then he would begin all over again and achieve his goal another way.

He lived like this for one year, two years, three years, occasionally taking a break from this strict routine of life but more often than not he kept at it. Guiding his imagination, he freed himself from the involuntary hallucinations. Only occasionally did fits of sleeplessness and visions, those faces, descend on him, and then he would look at the vent and consider how he would strengthen the rope and how he would make the noose and hang himself. But these fits did not continue long. He overcame them.

He went on living in this way for almost seven years. When his prison term ended, and they sent him to hard labor, he was fully fresh and healthy, and in full possession of his mental powers.

XI.

THEY BROUGHT HIM alone, as an especially important prisoner, not letting him communicate with anyone else. It was only in the Krasnoyarsk prison that he managed for the first time to enter into communication with the other political prisoners who were also being sent to hard labor. There were six—two women and four men. They were all young people of a new mold, unknown to Mezhenetsky. They were the revolutionaries of the next generation, his successors, so they interested him especially. Mezhenetsky expected to meet people who were following in his footsteps, whom it behooved to value highly everything that had been done by their predecessors, and especially by him, Mezhenetsky. He prepared to treat them fondly and condescendingly. But to his unpleasant surprise, these youngsters not only did not regard him as their predecessor and teacher but treated him as it were condescendingly, bypassing or excusing his old-fashioned views. In the opinion of these new revolutionaries, everything that Mezhenetsky and his friends had done, all their attempts to incite the peasants and, mainly, the terror and all the assassinations: Governor Kropotkin, Mezentsov[14] and Alexander II himself—all that was a series of mistakes. It had only led to the reaction that triumphed under Alexander III and turned society backward, almost back to serfdom. The path to liberation of the people, in the opinion of these new ones, was completely different.

Over the course of two days and almost two nights the arguments between Mezhenetsky and his new acquaintances did not stop. One person in particular, the leader of them all, "Roman," as everyone called him, using just his first name, was painfully offensive to Mezhenetsky, with his unwavering conviction of his own rectitude and his condescending, even mocking, rejection of all the past activity of Mezhenetsky and his comrades.

The people, as understood by Roman, was a coarse mob, a herd of cattle, and, standing at its present level of development, nothing could be done with it. All efforts to elevate the population of the Russian village amounted to trying to set fire to stone or ice. It was necessary to educate the people, it was necessary to habituate them to solidarity, and this could be done only by massive industrialization and the socialist organization of the people that grew from it. Not only did the people not need land, it made them conservative and slavish. Not only at home but also in Europe. And he cited from memory authoritative opinions and statistics. The people needed to be freed from the land. And the sooner this was done, the better. The more of them that went into the factories, the more land the capitalists gathered up, the more they oppressed them, the better. Only the solidarity of the people could destroy despotism, and principally capitalism, and this solidarity might be achieved only through unions and worker corporations; that is, only when the masses stopped being landowners and became proletarians.

Mezhenetsky argued and grew heated. One of the women especially irritated him; she was not bad looking, a brunette with bushy hair and brightly glittering eyes, who, sitting at the window as if not taking part in the conversation, occasionally put in a word to confirm Roman's contentions, or only laughed contemptuously at the words Mezhenetsky said.

[14] These were real-life political figures assassinated by revolutionaries in 1879, 1878, and 1881, respectively.

"Is it really possible to remake all the agricultural people into factory hands?" said Mezhenetsky.

"Why not?" Roman objected. "It's a general economic law."

"How do we know that the law is universal?" said Mezhenetsky.

"Read Kautsky,"[15] the brunette put in with a contemptuous smile.

"Even if this is admitted," said Mezhenetsky, "(and I am not admitting it), if the people are remade into proletarians, why do you think that they will slot into the form predetermined for them by you?"

"Because it has been scientifically established," put in the brunette, turning away from the window.

When they spoke about the form the activity would have to take to accomplish this goal, the disagreement became even greater. Roman and his friends insisted on need to train an army of workers to effect the transition of the peasants into factory hands, and to propagandize socialism among the workers. And not only not to fight openly with the government but instead use it to achieve their goals. Mezhenetsky, though, said that it was necessary to fight the government directly, to terrorize it, and that the government was stronger and cleverer than they. "You won't trick the government; it will trick you. We propagandized the people and also fought the government."

"And you did so much!" the brunette said ironically.

"Yes, I think that a direct fight with the government is a waste of strength," said Roman.

"The First of March—a waste of strength!"[16] Mezhenetsky yelled. "We sacrificed ourselves, our lives, and you sit calmly in your homes enjoying life, and all you do is preach."

"We're not enjoying life all that much," said Roman calmly, glancing at his comrades, and he chuckled victoriously with his uninfectious but loud, distinctive, self-confident laugh.

Shaking her head, the brunette smiled contemptuously.

"We're not enjoying life all that much," said Roman. "And if we're sitting here, we owe it to that reaction—the reaction produced specifically by the First of March."

Mezhenetsky went quiet. He felt that he was choking with anger, and he went out into the corridor.

---

[15] Karl Kautsky was an editor and author promoting Marxism.
[16] On March 1, 1881, revolutionaries assassinated Tsar Alexander II.

XII.

TRYING TO CALM himself, Mezhenetsky began walking back and forth in the corridor. The doors of the cells were open until the evening roll-call. A tall blond prisoner, with a face whose kindliness was not disrupted by a half-shaved head, approached Mezhenetsky.

"A prisoner there in our cell saw your honor. 'Summon him to me,' he says."

"Which prisoner?"

"He goes by the name 'Tobacco Power.' He's a little old man, of the Old Believers. 'Summon to me,' he says, 'that person.' Meaning your honor, that is."

"But where is he?"

"Right there, in our cell. 'Hail that gentleman,' he says."

Mezhenetsky went with the prisoner to a small cell with cots, on which the prisoners were sitting and lying down.

On bare boards, under a gray prison robe, on the edge of a cot, lay that same Old Believer, the old man who seven years before had come to Mezhenetsky to ask about Svetlogub. The old man's face was pale, completely dried and wrinkled now, his hair was still as thick, his sparse beard was completely gray and protruded upward. His eyes were light blue, kind and attentive. He was lying on his back and was evidently feverish; his cheekbones showed a sickly flush.

Mezhenetsky approached him.

"What do you want?" he asked.

With difficulty the old man raised up on his elbow and offered his small, dry, trembling hand. Gathering himself to speak, almost swaying, he was breathing heavily, and, struggling for breath, said quietly, "You didn't reveal it to me back then, God be with you, but I will reveal it to everyone."

"What are you revealing?"

"About the Lamb … about the Lamb I reveal … that young man was with the Lamb. It is said: 'The Lamb shall overcome them … and they that are with him are called, and chosen, and faithful.'"

"I don't understand," said Mezhenetsky.

"Understand in your spirit. The kings shall receive dominion from the Beast. But the Lamb shall overcome them."

"Which kings?" said Mezhenetsky.

"'And there are seven kings: five are fallen, and one is, and the other is not yet come'—that means he has not come—'and when he cometh, he must continue a short space'—that means, his end will come … Understand?"

Mezhenetsky shook his head, thinking that the old man was rambling and that his words were senseless. The prisoners, his cellmates, thought so too. The prisoner with the shaved head who had summoned Mezhenetsky approached him and, nudging him with his elbow to draw Mezhenetsky's attention, winked toward the old man.

"He prates and prates, our Tobacco Power," he said. "But about what, he himself doesn't know."

So they thought, both Mezhenetsky and his cellmates, looking at the old man. But the old man well knew what he was saying, and what he was saying had for him a clear and deep meaning. The meaning was that evil would not long hold sway, that the Lamb, with goodness and humility, would conquer all; the Lamb would wipe away every tear, and that there would be neither weeping nor sickness nor death. And he felt that this was already coming about, was coming about throughout the whole world, because this was already coming about in his soul, enlightened by its proximity to death.

"Come soon! Amen. Come, Lord Jesus!" he said, and gave a slight, meaningful and, as it seemed to Mezhenetsky, crazy smile.

XIII.

"THERE HE IS, the representative of the people," thought Mezhenetsky, leaving the old man. "And this one's the best of them. And so benighted! They"—he was referring to Roman and his friends—"say: 'With such a people as they are now, it's impossible to do anything.'"

Mezhenetsky had at one time been doing his revolutionary work among the people, and he knew all about what he called the Russian peasant's inertia; he had met soldiers, both serving and retired, and he knew their dull-witted faith in the oath, in their need to be obedient, and the impossibility of affecting them by reason. He knew all this but had never drawn from this knowledge the conclusion that inescapably flowed from it. The conversation with the new revolutionaries upset and irritated him.

"They say that all we did, that Khalturin, Kibalchich, and Perovskaya[17] did, all that was unnecessary, even harmful, that it elicited Alexander III's reaction, and that thanks to it, the people were convinced that all the revolutionary activity came from the landowners,

---

[17] These were revolutionaries who were hanged for their part in assassinating Tsar Alexander II.

that they killed the tsar because he had taken away their serfs. What nonsense! What a lack of understanding and what impertinence to think like that!" he thought, continuing to pace the corridor.

All the cells were closed, except one, the one where the new revolutionaries were. Approaching it, Mezhenetsky heard the laughter of the one he hated, the brunette, and Roman's crackling, decisive voice. They were obviously talking about him. Mezhenetsky stopped to listen.

Roman said, "Not understanding the economic laws, they did not realize what they were doing. And the larger part here was ..."

Mezhenetsky could not and did not want to hear what the larger part was, but it was not necessary for him to know that. Just that person's tone of voice showed the full contempt that these people felt toward him, Mezhenetsky, the hero of the revolution, who had ruined twelve years of his life for this cause.

And there arose in Mezhenetsky's soul such a fearsome anger as he had never before experienced. The anger at everyone, at everything, at the entire senseless world, in which only people resembling animals, like that old man with his Lamb, and like the executioners and jailers, half-men, half-beasts, and those impudent, self-confident, stillborn doctrinarians.

The guard on duty came in and led the political women to the women's half of the prison. Mezhenetsky turned back to the far end of the corridor so as not to encounter them. Returning, the watchman locked the door of the new politicals and asked Mezhenetsky to enter his cell. Mezhenetsky automatically obeyed, but asked him not to lock the door.

Returning to his cell, Mezhenetsky lay on the cot, his face to the wall.

"Did I really lay waste to all my strengths—my energy, will-power, genius—in vain?" (He never counted anyone higher in intellectual qualities than himself.) "Laid waste to no avail!" He remembered not long ago, when he was already on the road to Siberia, the letter he received from Svetlogub's mother reproaching him in her stupid, womanly way, as he thought, for having ruined her son, for attracting him into the terrorist party. When he received the letter, he had only smiled contemptuously: What could this stupid woman understand about the goals that faced him and Svetlogub? But now, remembering the letter and Svetlogub's sweet, trusting, enthusiastic personality, he reflected first on him, and then on himself. Had his whole life been a mistake? He closed his eyes and wanted to sleep, but he suddenly felt with horror that the state of mind he had experienced in his first month at the Peter and Paul Fortress had returned. There was again the pain in the crown of his head, again the faces, big-mouthed, shaggy, horrible against a dark, spangled background, and again the figures presenting themselves to his open eyes. A new thing was a shaven-headed criminal in gray pants swinging above him. And again, by a concatenation of ideas, he began seeking a vent from which he might fasten a rope.

An unbearable anger demanding outward display burned Mezhenetsky's heart. He could not sit still, he could not calm down, he could not drive off the thoughts.

"How?" he began posing the question to himself. "Slice an artery? I won't know how. Hang myself? That's the simplest, to be sure."

He remembered the rope tied around the bundle of firewood that lay in the corridor. "Stand on the firewood or on the stool. The guard walks the corridor. But he will fall asleep or go out. It'll be necessary to wait and then I'll take the rope and fasten it to the vent."

Standing by his door, Mezhenetsky heard the guard's steps in the corridor and when the guard occasionally walked off to the far end, he glanced through the little window in the door. The guard still hadn't gone out and still hadn't fallen asleep. Mezhenetsky listened avidly to the sounds of his footsteps and waited.

At this time in that cell where the sick old man was, barely illuminated by a smoky lamp, and amid the sleepy nocturnal sounds, the breathing, the muttering, the groans, the snores, the coughs, the greatest thing in the world was taking place. The Old Believer was dying, and to his spiritual gaze was revealed everything that he had so passionately sought and desired his entire life. In the midst of a blinding radiance, he saw the Lamb in the form of the radiant young man, and a vast multitude of people of all nations were standing before him in white garments, and they all rejoiced, and there was no longer any evil on earth. Everything was fulfilled; the old man knew this, both in his soul and in all the world, and he felt great joy and peace.

But for the people in his cell, what happened was that the old man wheezed loudly, the wheezing before death, and his neighbor woke up and awakened the others; and when the wheezing ended, and the old man went quiet and grew cold, his cellmates began pounding on the door.

The guard unlocked the door and went in to the prisoners. Ten minutes later, two prisoners brought out the dead body and bore it down to the morgue. The guard went out behind them and locked the door behind him. The corridor was left empty.

"Lock it, lock it," thought Mezhenetsky, following from his door everything that was happening. "Don't prevent me from quitting this entire absurd horror."

Mezhenetsky no longer felt that inner horror that had tormented him before. He was absorbed by a single thought: that nothing should prevent him from fulfilling his intention.

With a trembling heart, he approached the bundle of firewood, untied the rope, pulled it out from under the wood and, looking around at the door, brought it into his cell. In the cell, he climbed atop the stool and looped the rope over the vent. Having tied both ends of the rope, he tightened the knot, and from the doubled rope made a noose. The noose was too low. He retied the rope, made the noose again, fitted it around his neck, and, anxiously listening and looking around at the door, stepped onto the stool, slipped his head into the noose, adjusted it, and, pushing off the stool, hung there …

Only during the morning rounds did the guard see Mezhenetsky, who was standing on legs bent at the knees next to the stool that lay on its side. They took him out of the noose. The warden ran in and, learning that Roman was a doctor, called him to help the strangled man.

All the usual means to revive him were tried, but Mezhenetsky did not revive.

Mezhenetsky's body was brought to the morgue and was laid on a cot alongside the body of the Old Believer.

(1906)
Translated by Bob Blaisdell